STUCK BETWEEN TWO WORLDS

by

LISA PARKES

"Nothing in life is to be feared, it is only to be understood. Now is the time to understand more, so that we may fear less." *Marie Curie*

An inspiring and heart-warming story *for the lost souls among us who feel like we don't quite belong. The endless search for that special friend who truly understands, and that peaceful place we can call home.*

Really good fun and lots to discover! *I loved the powerful, positive messages in this book. The life lessons given throughout were well explained and cleverly woven into the story. It made me think about how I could use them too because I could see how they were really helping Ruby. I loved all the characters and the colourful scenes of the magical world you created.*

A magical adventure story with a twist! *I really liked the emotional side of this book, the steps taken to address the tangle of feelings and the resolution once they are dealt with. I think it will give children a working tool in their own lives. I like Ruby. She is a smart little girl with a kind heart. You really want her to succeed, but you wonder where she will end up. It's fascinating to watch her blossom, as she has to unlearn so much and follow her heart.*

A real joy to read! *I found the way the author used different characters to describe different emotions really interesting and innovative. A lot of thought, work and research has clearly gone into the book. I really felt a connection to the characters and how they felt. The book was relatable but also not too full on. It was certainly a gentler way of saying 'We can talk about mental health and feelings' instead of saying 'There's something wrong with you! You need help!' Nettle stood out for me as she represented my mum, being there for me and listening to my problems whenever I have them.*

To all the wonderful Wildhearts: From my Wild Heart to yours. Don't settle for black and white! Never doubt who you truly are. Unleash your mighty magic and use this book to find your way to live life in full colour.

Please help other children find this book so they can learn too!

If you leave me a review on Amazon, then more children will get to find out about this book! I want to help them and I know you do too. I would love to know what you think, so be sure to leave me a review.

PROLOGUE

I know a place that we can go, it's called The Wilderness don't you know?
The soul of The Wildnerness is colourful and bright, there are no sides, no black or white.
Different is how you were born to be, you're not meant to be the same as me!

The call of The Wilderness is gentle but strong, the place to dance your own sweet song.
The wisdom of The Wilderness is intuitive and true, follow your heart, it knows what to do.
The scent of The Wilderness is relaxing and calm, nature's beauty reassures that you will come to no harm.
The promise of The Wilderness is of camaraderie, where Wildhearts connect over rose petal tea.
These are the friendships that last for all time, the togetherness and sharing of what is yours and mine.
There is no meanness or cruelty, only fun, kindness and integrity.

The love of the Wilderness is warm and snug, it's a safe resting place, like a neverending hug.
It reminds you that it's not just you, who feels left out, lonely and blue.
It shows you the magic that lives inside, it doesn't make you want to hide
Your angries, your mistakes or your sads, those things have never been shameful, naughty or bad.
It shines a light from head to toe, so you can find yourself at peace wherever you go.

The people of the Wilderness are just like you, other Wildhearts who at first, worried they were wrong or mad, but deep inside they were truly sad that those around them could not see, the fire in your heart, your honesty.
There's nothing more painful than being misunderstood—the constant yearning to be seen as good.
You see, lovely Wildheart, your feelings aren't wrong, they're the part of you that makes you strong.
Listen to them and what they have to say, they want to help you find your way.

Sensitive, kind, yet fiercely brave, you're a protector, a helper, you want to save
other children and animals who feel lost and small, you fight hard to make it right for them all.
But now it's time to stop and step back; to end your struggle with all this lack.
To see yourself in your sparkling glory; you'll uncover it easily when you read my story.
Let's venture to the Wilderness right now, and together we can discover how
being you is amazing really, when you find the right people who love you so dearly.

INDEX

CHAPTER 1

THE CROSSROADS

'Are you ready?' she whispered as she peered through the window from the garden.

Together, we stood on the patio, watching a man resting in his cosy armchair. His mouth was slightly open, glasses on the end of his nose, fast asleep. He was dressed in a red polo shirt and leather moccasin slippers poked out from under his faded jeans. Next to them on the floor was a half-finished mug of coffee and the daily newspaper.

I swallowed and stared at him. I could feel the tears bubbling up. My lunch had turned into rocks weighing heavily in the pit of my tummy. I tried to speak. There was no sound. Big fat tears dripped onto my t-shirt. It was my all-time favourite—soft cotton with a big rainbow, which was now glistening with sadness amongst the colourful sequins.

I had longed for this day. Longed to be with people who understood me and who accepted me for me. I hadn't realised that my freedom came at a price.

That feeling in my tummy really hurt. Love didn't hurt. That's what Nettie had taught me, but I'd never been very good at goodbyes. 'Why do they call them that anyway?' I would ask. 'There's nothing good about them'. *Or is there? Could they lead to happy hellos*?

I was angry. I turned to Nettie. 'I don't want this! Don't make me choose!' More tears bubbled up.

'Ah, Ruby,' said Nettie, her arm gently resting on my shoulder. 'We're here. We've got you.'

I raised my eyebrows and bit my lip trying to stop myself from crying, but I couldn't. Between sobs I muttered, 'This is too hard. This is so much harder than I ever imagined.'

Then I did one of those big snorty sniffs and Nettie passed me a tissue. No doubt she was wondering how she was going to clean the snot encrusted sequins. I mean, nobody wants that job.

'It *is* really hard, lovely Girl.' She turned and folded down her wings like an umbrella behind her.

'You're doing what's right for you. He can come and find you when he's ready.'

I stared down at my leather sandals. They had superglued themselves to the patio. That stuff is strong. I wouldn't budge. Heavy and tense, I looked across at Nettie. She was patting the curls on top of her head. She smiled at me. I could feel her kindness as she straightened her flowery crown and jumped down from the giant plant pot where she had been sitting.

'He won't come,' I said defeated. 'He is happy here. I don't make him happy.'

She moved in closer for a hug. 'That's not your job, remember? You can't make him happy. He has a choice. We all have to make choices.'

'Yes, I know. I know that my choices have consequences too,' I sighed. 'What if he is never ready?' I asked.

'He is free to change his mind at any time, but if he doesn't or he can't ... well' her voice trailed off. She put her finger under my chin and tilted my head up to meet her gaze. She smiled. 'Then he will miss out on the joy of knowing you. I've had so much fun with you, Poppet. His loss will be our gain.'

As Queen of the Wildhearts, Nettie brought hundreds of lost souls to The Wilderness. This was her warm and welcoming homeland where she had beamed light into their darkness and helped them to become happy again. The darkness can get you like that. It seeps into everything making it a big confused mess. Lost souls in the darkness are like necklaces tangled up together in your jewellery box. It takes patience and time to free each one from the enmeshed clump, so they can exist independently.

She smiled again. ‘He never really knew you, did he? He never really took the time to get to know you like we do. I want to cry for him because he is suffering the biggest loss of all.’

‘He doesn’t know that, Nettie, does he? He doesn’t think I’m wonderful. He thinks I’m a troublemaker. It’s not fair. I can’t ... I can’t leave. He is my family.’ My tears fell hot and angry.

‘She is your family too,’ she nodded her head towards the kitchen window. There was my Mum stood at the sink washing up. Wearing yellow gloves to protect her manicured fingernails, she stared ahead of her, zombie-like, as if she wasn’t really there.

‘You’re not worried about leaving her are you?’

'Nope.' I clenched my jaw defiantly. Thinking about her made me even angrier.

'What is family, lovely Girl?' asked Nettie. 'He has a daughter he doesn't really know. Just like his father never knew him. Is that what family is? It sounds more like heartbreak to me.'

I thought about this and I wondered if she was right—that without somebody to show them the way, families just repeat what has gone before them. Nettie had led me to the wonderful world of The Wildnerness and opened my eyes to a very different way of living. Now I was at a crossroads, and I'm going to tell you how I got here.

Ever since the day Nettie found me crying in my room, she had brought all the questions in my head to life and helped me make sense of them. She had given them a voice and because she listened, she made it so much easier for me to hear myself. Loudly and clearly without doubting, she was like a refreshing ice pop on a hot summer's day. Her bubbly energy and sweet nature was an utter joy to be around. Her calm and peaceful presence had helped me to feel safe enough to step out into the big wide world and adventure with her.

It was some time ago when one dusky evening, Nettie appeared seemingly from nowhere—as if by magic. Well, she *was* magical. She had wings, didn't she? She was powerful and full of love. Not powerful like my parents in a 'We will make you obey' controlling way, but in a soft and gentle way. She listened. She understood. She was firm and fair and consistently calm. There were no surprises with her. She showed up the same over and over again. I knew what I was getting and so I could easily put my trust in her.

I had been laying on my bed staring down at the floral duvet. The pastel flowers matched the wallpaper in my picture-perfect bedroom. That was my life, picture perfect to the outside world, but on the inside just one big angry mess.

Angry messes were my speciality. For the third time that week, I'd been sent to my room for my back talk. I was a Chatty Patty with far too much to say for myself. It usually happened at tea-time. 'The witching hour' my Mum called it because she said children were ghastly when they were tired and hungry. I think she was talking about herself—she could be quite ghastly too, you know?

I had been sitting on my windowsill staring up at the wire netting above the guttering. Below was the moss-covered patio with terracotta pots and flower beds. The chicken wire was wrapped around the guttering. It stopped the pigeons from nesting in the roof. I looked out of the window at the big garden. A little to my right was a tall fir tree and in front of me lay a lush green lawn. Its perfectly mown stripes were the handy work of my Dad, who took immense pride in keeping it so. Beyond that were more fir trees and beyond that, what we called 'the end of the garden', there was a rickety shed and overgrown vegetable patch.

I could totally relate to those pigeons having to stay stuck on red alert so they didn't get enmeshed in the wire. *They* said it was to keep me safe—except it wasn't to keep me safe. It was to keep me small and quiet. Slight problem—I didn't do anything quietly. I had a huge explosive temper that was sparked by unfairness, lies, and my parents. I was too much. Yes, *they* made me very angry. They didn't understand. They were impossible people. You say black, they say white. I think we all know people like that. On some days, nothing I did was ever right and if for a minute I did get it right, I couldn't quite trust it would be okay because it wouldn't be long before they were impossible again.

Nettie said that impossible people only saw things in black and white terms. It was all or nothing.

Right or wrong—they were always right, and you were always wrong! My parents were never wrong. Even when they were wrong, they were right. There was no grace, no compassion, no apology, or empathy. Somebody else had to take the hit and be the bad guy. It was crazy. I wanted to scream, and I did scream a lot. Nettie went on to explain that impossible people living in their black and white world missed out on all the colours of the rainbow. Ah, I love rainbows! Did I mention that I love them? Rainbows were my sign of hope. That after living in a black and white world for so long, I longed for colour. Eventually, after hanging with Nettie and her friends in The Wilderness, colour burst into my life in more ways than I could have ever imagined.

I looked in at my black and white world at my black and white family who didn't really get me. It sounds absurd, but I often wondered if I was born into the wrong family. Did they mix me up with another baby at the hospital? Would my real family come and find me one day? Where were Mr and

Mrs Technicolour? Surely they were still searching for their bonny baby?

Or maybe, I was born into my family to colour in the black and white. It was a lot for one small person to take on. Even with all my big bold colour and sparkly smiles, I'm not sure I could do this job alone. I think that's why Nettie came to help me. You can imagine my surprise, the day Nettie appeared. It was like the missing piece to my puzzle. The loving and belonging I had been thirsting for.

CHAPTER 2

GETTING TO KNOW YOU

I don't think we've met. My name is Ruby and I'm 9 and a half years old. I'll be ten on Valentine's Day. St. Valentine is the patron saint of love. Being born on a day that's all about love makes so much sense to a girl who had to search hard for it. I was born two weeks early and even now, I hate being late.

Lots of people think I'm older. I don't blame them. I have a very wise head on these young shoulders. Once, a funny old lady stopped my Mum in the supermarket and told her that I was an old soul. She claimed that I had been here many lifetimes before and I was a time traveller. I think that's a bit bananas and I'm not really sure if I believe it! One thing I do know for sure —I'm a Wildheart. I have a feeling you're one too. Once you've read this book, you'll feel indescribably good inside—like you've just *WHOOSHED* down a great big water slide with your hands in the air.

Even better, once you read it, you can't unknow it. It will speak to your heart—your Wild Heart. You won't forget it, but why would you want to when it's the very thing you've been searching for all this time. You're home. Put your feet up! You belong here. You're going to find your place in the world. I totally understand that searching feeling. Not like the missing sock that never made it through the wash, or the coins that have fallen down the back of the sofa. No, this was more of a hole, a feeling of emptiness and no matter what you did, it couldn't be filled.

So, I want to take you to The Wonderful Wilderness, where you will discover what you need to live your best life. It's not something you learn at school and sometimes not even your parents know. It's not their fault. They can only give you what they have inside of them. Together, we're going to pay attention to your sad, hurty, and angry bits. You'll see. Despite what you may think or have been taught, all your feelings have important messages for you to understand.

Every moment you spend with this story will ease your bads, mads or sads. For every step you take towards knowing who you truly are, your life and the world will be a better place. No matter what anyone tells you, the world is definitely a better place with you in it. As you feel less sad, hurty, and angry, you will grow in confidence and you will inspire others to do the same. You'll show others the way, because that's what Wildhearts were born to do—to lead and to teach.

Now you're asking, 'How do I know if I'm a Wildheart?'

For as long as I can remember, I thought I was weird. I thought I was strange and not like other children. Not that I thought I was special, but more like I was wrong. I was wrong and bad. Now that is a pretty yucky recipe and feels like poo. Being wrong and bad will take you to all sorts of nasty places in your head. None of them are real or true. They are simply places in your head, but it's quite hard to escape, and not because your head is attached to the rest of your body. It's your brain—it believes whatever you tell it is true. So, if you're making yourself wrong and feeding your brain negative critical and mean thoughts all day long, it will feel like poo in your body! You're meant to feel safe inside your own body. It houses the spirit of you—it's the place where nobody is allowed to go unless you say so. Your spirit is the essence of who you are and that's precious. There is only one of you and the world needs your preciousness. You were born to do great things and so was I, but people had invaded my inner world without my permission. Nettie said I was like a soft, white lychee without a skin. I didn't come with my bumpy greenish pink skin to protect me from the body snatchers.

I didn't quite feel entirely safe because *they* were quite unpredictable. What was right and what was wrong? Was I good or was I bad? I am the bossy big sister and I have very short ginger hair. I could be mistaken for a boy—this was before Ed Sheeran and Prince Harry made it cool. I have sparkly blue eyes and a pale freckly face. The heat gives me a rash and I burn easily. I have big red lips and my ears are pierced with gold studs. My skin turns pink without a head to toe coating of thick sunscreen lotion. Urgh, that's a sweaty mess let me tell you. Sun times were certainly not fun times. When the sun is out, I prefer to be under the shady trees or stay indoors. I sit on the red wiry carpet of my playroom and prop myself against a flowery cushion or two. I make myself comfortable by the window so I can see outside. The rabbit, Snowy keeps me company on rainy days. I make book tunnels for him and the guinea pig to run through. The guinea pig is called Squirt—let's not get into the story behind his name right now!

When this room was first decorated, my Mum let me choose the salmon pink walls. I'm happy amongst the wooden toy boxes and rows of books peeping out from the shelved walls. I can lose myself easily in books. As I read, I imagine the story unfolding in colour. It's almost like I'm running a movie from the black screen inside my mind. Your imagination is the coolest place on earth and it's all yours. Nobody can tell you what to think. Nobody can get in there and crawl around. It's private and it's fun. So, because the outside world isn't always a safe place for me to be, I prefer living in my head. That is my safe space and, I'm comforted by daydreams, drifting off to make up stories and poems. I love to doodle and colour. I'm not the world's best artist, but I create anyway because it helps me feel better. I need that comfort because I am way too hard on myself sometimes.

Our house has so much space to play and explore. Pretend games are my thing because I get to make my imagination a reality. Once you bring the ideas out of your head, they take on a life of their own. You don't know where they will end up, but you know they will be fun, and you know there will be laughter. I like to make believe our hallway is a hotel reception. I welcome my doll guests and furry animals. I check them into their rooms with a twinkly smile. TICK! TICK! TICK! goes my red pen.

'Here are your keys Madame. You're in the Blue Room. Go to the end of the corridor and turn left,' I confidently inform my trendy Barbie who is decked out in cowboy boots and a pink hat. I spend ages styling out my dolls and deciding what I want them to wear. I like bright colours and things that match.

Sometimes, I pretend to be a Librarian. I love the strong feeling of stamping the books with return dates. Click! Thud! Click! Thud! firmly onto the page. I think I'm good at being in charge. It suits me. I'm not sure it suits my parents. They seem to want to be in charge and I don't like being told what to do. I can't wait to be a grown up and then it will be my turn!

'Thank you, Bobby Beans, that one is due back in a week. It's a good one, I've read it myself.' I proudly tell my bean bag bodied friend. His plastic head smiles approvingly.

My Mum lets us have the whole run of the house when it comes to pretend play. In the summer, that extends to the garden with a huge red paddling pool. The rules are that we must tidy away when we have finished. When there's no school, we stay out until the sun disappears behind the trees. The garden goes to sleep in the leafy shadows, the light dims and the grass feels damp under our feet. We sit silent, wrapped in our swimming towels. The scent of dusk drifts in from the grassy edges. Enclosed by the pink flower beds, the rose petals cherish the moment with us. It's getting cold but we don't want the fun to end.

'Bathtime!' my Mum beckons from the back door. She stands on the patio with her rubber gloves on. We've enjoyed our perfect picnic tea in between the straight lines of the neatly mowed lawn. I hope the squelchy bits, where we've been splashing about, dry out by the morning so nobody gets told off. Or maybe it will save my Dad the job of watering it. It's time to go in and have a bath.

While tidying up my playroom, I like to make sure the toys are all together. I cannot bear to see any of them left out or without a friend. I feel mean when I turn out the light because I know how they feel in the darkness. I know they need each other for company and to feel safe. That's why I arrange them all close together. I put Barbie and Cindy in their house so they can go to the kitchen to cook supper and sleep in their beds. I hope when I leave, they have a lot of fun, or at least a rest so they are ready to play again the next day.

I put the books back on the shelves and breathe in their papery goodness. I've read every book from cover to cover and often more than once. Each time, I find something new. I often overlook words and I read super fast. I can't wait to get to the end and find out what happens. I don't want to run out of time, and I find it hard to not know things. I'm more excited about learning new things and finding answers to satisfy all the questions inside my busy brain. It's impatient and won't be kept waiting.

My brain is like a zany quiz master that's had too much sugar. It quickly demands to know the answers to everything. It's never quiet. I wish it would shut up. I get tired, but I can't sleep. The only thing that helps me to feel safe and happy at bedtime, is reading. I can't sleep until calm and peace flood my body. I watch the clock. The numbers change and I start to frantically count on my fingers how many hours are left before I have to get up for school.

I'm alone in the darkness. I don't have a teddy or a blankie. I think of my toys downstairs in the playroom. I wonder what they are up to and hope they're okay. I've never had a dummy and even though I sucked my thumb for a while, I stopped. I wonder if that's why I find it hard to fall asleep. I don't have anything to soothe my busy brain. Nothing works except the books.

I'm terrified of the dark. The hall light shines through the crack in the half-shut bedroom door. It doesn't feel safe completely open and I've got my back to it. I sleep on my tummy with one arm under my pillow and one eye open. I hear every sound in the garden below my bedroom window and I wonder who is coming to get me. As I'm drifting off, my legs jerk me awake like an electric shock and I become more and more frustrated.

My Mum does a guided tour of the doors and windows to prove that we're safe. 'Everything is locked. We're here. Nobody can get in.' She listens to my worries. I don't feel reassured. She wants to do her pile of ironing and be with her friend. I feel like I'm irritating her. On a Wednesday Auntie Pam comes over. They've been friends since school.

They drink gallons of tea and talk boring grown-up talk. Pam lives in London, but she can't drive. Pam's husband, Bert is her chauffeur. Bert is quite serious, and he has a grey moustache. He is a good listener and when you talk to him, his reply to most things is, 'This is true'. I love Bert because I'm obsessed with the truth and I love detective programmes. He watches those on TV whilst he works on his computer. Bert likes to be on his own and he doesn't seem to worry about much. Bert is a Policeman and he is the reason I sleep well on Wednesdays.

My Dad meets up with his old school friends on a Wednesday night to play cards, but he tells us he is going to see a man about a dog. Sometimes when I question my Dad about the dog, he replies, 'To make your tongue wag.' I want to say, 'Seriously Dad! What are you talking about?' but I don't. There is no dog, but we do have a cat called Tom. I'm pretty sure we won't be getting a dog any time soon. We can't even remember to clean and feed the rabbit as it is. I love Tom. He's a big fluffy tabby that belonged to my Dad when he was a boy. Tom has these beautiful eyes that seem to know you. I love Tom even when he comes and blasts his stinky cat food breath in my face. It's not his fault he can't talk. I mean how else is he supposed to wake me up for breakfast?

My Dad laughs at me and teases me about the darkness. It's not funny. The fear takes over my whole body. I freeze. There is evil in our garden and I can't tell my Dad that because he doesn't take me seriously. I know that something is coming to get me. Actually, I think there is a Shadow Man living in the bathroom. Our yellow bathroom—we have a blue one too—is halfway up the stairs on the corner so you can't miss it. The Shadow Man has a black cloak and tall hat and he lives in the toilet. We'll talk more about him later. He has taught me to do the quickest wees ever. Isn't that crazy?

Late one night, my Dad bet me ten pounds that I couldn't go out in the garden to feed Snowy. Snowy's hutch was in an old cobwebby shed right at the end of our garden. It was easy to forget about cleaning and feeding him because he was far away hidden behind a row of fir trees. Snowy shared the shed with the lawnmower and loads of gardening tools. The weed killer gave it a bitter smell that was a mix of strong ground coffee and musty dry soil. To be honest, I didn't like it much in the shed during the day. So I certainly wasn't going to venture there in the middle of the night, was I?

I so badly wanted to be right and prove to my Dad that I could do it. I would loiter on the patio outside the back door and then look back at my Dad waiting inside. He was pointing and laughing. 'Go on then!' he mouthed motioning with his head towards the pitch-black garden. He raised his eyebrows. That was his disappointed look. It was usually followed by a shaking of his head and walking away.

Nobody, aside from my family, really knows about my Dad's other side. In fact, most people love him and know him as a jolly man who suffers at the hands of the five women he lives with. He can be a lot of fun. I love it when he gives me a flying angel—he lifts me up onto his broad shoulders and I sit there while he walks around. It's not scary, I hold onto his head, and I get to see how everything looks from up high in his world. He doesn't suffer. He lives like a King feasting on my Mum's delicious home cooked meals, and he eats a lot of fruit cake and digestive biscuits. He doesn't have to lift a finger, apart from work six days a week and that's alright by him because as he will tell you, he loves to work. He's crazy bonkers in love with it. I've been to my Dad's Butcher's shop and I'm not that impressed with it. They put sawdust down to soak up the blood and they have their own Butcher language which is mostly swear words spelt backwards! You can work it out if you're switched on like me! Butchers carry cleavers and sharp knives. It seems inappropriate that they wear pristine white aprons when you think about all the animal carcasses and blood. It's a scary horror movie. I like the way my Dad smells, but I'm sure it's not everybody's favourite. Aftershave, sawdust and raw meat, but you know he's my Dad and people have strong smells which remind you of them. Smells are powerful. They can make your feelings stronger. When I smell the sawdust smell, I long to be close to my Dad.

My Dad works hard and leaves the house at 5 am to go to London. He doesn't come home until late. He's on his feet all day chopping meat and serving lots of customers. When he gets home, he's exhausted. He reads the paper and nods off in his cosy armchair. By Thursday, he's usually pretty grumpy—on a short fuse my Mum calls it—so we all do as we're told, because you really don't want to be around him when he blows.

Frozen by my fear of the darkness, I admit defeat. I miserably failed my bunny in the dark challenge. I couldn't do it. Not even for ten pounds which would have come in super handy. Think of all the sweets and magazines I could have bought with that. The Disappointed Dad Look got me as I waited shivering on the patio for him to open the back door. I was so cross and disappointed in myself. I hated to wimp out of a challenge. I also didn't want my Dad to feel like he had all the power. There were so many things I could do when I put my mind to them. Failure wasn't an option and I was a trier. It was unlike me to give up so easily. Maybe I wasn't ready to face the darkness this time. Once again, I came to the conclusion that its evil power was too strong for a small person like me.

'Can I try again another day?' I begged him.

'Naaaah you've made your bed,' he shook his head and rocked out another of his classic Dad lines. If you make a choice or a decision, why can't you change your mind? All these funny sayings made no sense to me. They aren't any comfort at all. Not much my Mum and Dad do comforts or reassures me. Why am I such a difficult child? Do I have something wrong with me? I get on their nerves a lot.

My Dad says I need constant reassurance. 'Don't keep on!' he would snap through gritted teeth. My Maths teacher, Mr Gregory told him at parents' evening that I had to get each sum right before I would start a new one. Mr Gregory wanted me to do a whole page of sums. I felt like I was bugging Mr Gregory too. My Dad agrees and thinks it's amusing. I don't. I hate Maths and I certainly don't like Mr Gregory. It's infuriating. *They* don't understand that I really want to do an excellent job. If I worked in a school I would make sure children were understood before anything else. You simply *cannot* learn when you're misunderstood. It takes a lot of energy to feel all your unhappiness and makes it hard to concentrate.

When I can't concentrate, I bite my nails until they bleed. I have other funny habits too. I wash my feet before I go to sleep. I like things to be symmetrical and neat. I can't settle unless the duvet is equal on both sides. If I snow angel from the middle of my mattress, I can check. I double check everything and like to plan ahead. Just in case something bad happens. It hasn't happened yet, but I need to be ready when it does. It's my job to look out for the bad things.

What will I wear tomorrow? What will I say? What will I do if I get it wrong or get into trouble? Maybe the sky will fall on my head! What do I have to remember to take in for swimming? Have I packed everything?

I love swimming under water. My dad is a strong swimmer and he taught me to swim like a dolphin. I can hold my breath for a whole length of the swimming pool. I love disappearing into the blurry depths. It's a peacefulness that surrounds me, like I'm hiding from the world and nobody will think to look there. It's not like the protection of the greasy sunscreen lotion they smother on me every holiday. It's a different kind of protection—it's more safe and secure. It's almost like an invisible hug. I often wish that feeling would last longer than being under the water.

I've been learning to dance since I was four. I go every Saturday morning and even though I hate wearing itchy, scratchy tights that fall down, I love the freedom to move with the music. *They* think I'm a show-off. I get nervy when I have to go on stage and perform. It's something I want to be better at. When I'm on stage, I feel like people are paying attention. Showtime feels powerful and the music makes it more so. I still haven't figured out how to overcome those pesky nerves. I don't think they are meant to go away completely because they keep you focused on doing your very best.

Make no mistake, I'm a little firecracker. I want to know it and do it all. I want to be noticed and I want them to pay attention. I tap dance, I crunch my crisps loudly, I play the piano and the recorder. I don't practise as often as I could do. *They* say I talk too much. I do talk a lot. I'm curious and I ask so many questions. I have so much I want to learn and want to tell people. It's sad when other people don't share my excitement when I've learnt something new.

They say I am too much. I think other people find me too much, too. They don't understand me. That's why I often get sent away to my room to calm down. They can't be around me when I'm like that. It's like I have all this power and I don't know what to do with it. Nobody actually said, but the message is loud and clear—it's not okay to be angry, and so I've decided that must be what makes me bad. I don't know if I am good like other children. I seem to be good at school but at home, I can't hold the bad in and it all comes tumbling out. My parents don't know what to do with it.

Until recently, I didn't truly understand what it meant to be a Wildheart. So, now it makes perfect sense to share it with you. I'm totally fired up. I'm so excited and I can't wait to tell you about my story. We're going to make amazing discoveries together. I'll show you how I went from lost and sad to happy and confident. Let's ignite that spark in you and light you up so the world can see you as you're meant to be. I can already tell that you're pretty amazing.

It's my wish for you because I really do know that it's a lonely place when you feel like you don't belong. You may even pretend to be somebody that you're not so you can fit in. You're not sure who to be but you really need a friend. You're looking for that one special friend who truly gets you. Well, here I am. You know it's okay because the need to belong in us is so strong. It's a powerful force because as humans, we're made to connect with one another. It helps to find the right kind of people, the ones who understand us and accept us as we are.

Are you ready then? What are we waiting for? Let's jump right in.

CHAPTER 3

LOST IN THE DARKNESS

Before Nettie appeared on the scene, I'd been lost. Have you ever felt that kind of miserable when it feels like a big grey cloud is following you everywhere? It's confusing when you don't know who you are. I mean, people say things like 'There's only one of you and you're unique.' Yeah, we're all special snowflakes and I'm not sure I'm one of those. I feel more like the slushy black snow that's left behind after everybody has finished having fun.

Nettie's arrival left me speechless. It takes a lot to silence me but I couldn't believe my eyes. I believe in magic and I read about magical creatures, but I didn't expect to be meeting one! The Tooth Fairy had left money under my pillow and disappeared without a trace. I thought you weren't meant to see magical beings. I was wrong because there she was — Nettie! She glided in with her wispy soft glow, making my sad cloud instantly disappear. Despite being small, she is the mighty Queen of the Wildhearts. She leads from her heart with kindness, and there isn't really anything about her that says royalty. She is humble and softly spoken in her simple dress and sandals. Even her crown is more of a flowery headdress, and it smells divine. Her little wings are paper thin and so delicate I didn't want to touch them. How else could I know that she was real? I haven't seen her fly. She has a crystal wand but her loving energy is her real superpower. It's a very strong, pure energy that stays with you long after she has left.

Nettie is a protector of Mother Earth and from the Fairy Forest Realm where she lives. She must get exhausted travelling backwards and forwards. I'm not sure if you can get jet lag travelling between the two dimensions. Not like we do. Nettie splits her time between her homeland and with children like me. We are the lost souls searching for that one special person to understand us. That is Nettie's job. She is the best at understanding.

I live in a big black and white house. It's a period house with a sweeping driveway. I called it

The Hologram House, because what you saw wasn't real. It was a 3D movie that wouldn't put up with vulnerability and had no time for badly-behaved children. Like a film is projected onto a cinema screen, the movie of our family left out any parts of life that were less than perfect. I mean that's most of life really isn't it? Living in the Hologram House was a mental assault course and there was no training programme. Some days you did it blindfolded or with your fingers crossed behind your back hoping somehow you would make it through the day without getting into trouble. Feeling secure and reassured about what was supposed to happen was a rare treat. There was a routine and homes for things, but it was mostly a crazy topsy turvy whirlwind that swept you up and spat you out. Even a mega observant Wildheart like me with super detective skills couldn't predict or stop the monumental levels of emotional chaos.

On some days you could snack before dinner was ready, on other days you would be sent to your room. On some days you could watch television or read all day, and nobody would even ask where you were. On other days you were lazy and not doing enough to get the jobs done. Right was left. Left was right. On Tuesday, the sky was green and the grass was blue. By Friday, it had all changed—the sky was blue and the grass was green.

'You stupid child! Why can't you just listen and do as you are told? Smack. Smack. Smack.

'I *am* listening, but you're not making any sense.'

'You're really testing my patience.' Slap. Slap. Slap. 'How many times do I have to tell you? Don't make me come upstairs and find it for you.'

Words you spoke were taken out of context, twisted and used against you at a later date. This was what made me doubt myself because I couldn't be sure of what I said or what had happened. Nobody noticed the lengths you went to, to try and get it right. Nobody noticed how much time and effort you made when you'd rather have been playing or having fun. Nobody knew that you frequently gazed into the night-time sky wishing on the twinkliest of stars that you could opt out of, or at least have a break from, the mental assault course that you had no recollection of signing up for.

I often wondered if there were lots of Rubys. I can be sure that there are definitely three of me. Let me introduce them to you. First up is *'Show*

Ruby' and as you would expect, she is the one who shows up for show time. This is the play of her family's life. It's her Mum and Dad's script. What the outside world gets to see is a good girl who goes to a top school and works hard. She helps her Mum and does tonnes of homework. She is smart —but she doesn't really believe that inside.

'Show Ruby' is expected to smile for photographs even when she feels sad. She is expected to hide her anger and disappointment. She is there to make other people laugh. She isn't allowed to make a fuss or say no. She is there to make her Mum and Dad proud and happy. She does what she is told. She isn't allowed to ask for what she wants because that's not part of the script. If you don't follow the script, that's selfish and makes the family look bad. *'Show Ruby'* doesn't need help anyway, because she can do it all by herself. She is strong and perfect. She doesn't fail or get it wrong.

'Show Ruby' is tough, but she's also wise and very aware of what is going on around her. She knows what other people are thinking and feeling. She can sense what they need, and she tries hard to make sure they get it. If she doesn't know, she will work it out.

Next up, I want you to meet *'Resting Ruby'* who buries herself in books and play. This Ruby is calm, thoughtful, and kind. She is sensitive with a fascinating imagination. It's richly colourful and where she drifts off to in Maths lessons, on long car journeys, or whilst watching TV. *'Resting Ruby'* likes to disappear into herself and get lost in her mind where nobody can find her. She is safe here and this is where she feels she has some power in her absurd world.

Last, but by no means least because she is a big part of me, meet *'Raging Ruby'*. She sniffs out danger or trouble instantly and she is fierce. She fights back and she is coming to get you. Fearless, this girl is on fire. She will stand up for what is right even if it means taking the wrap. She is more comfortable that way. She is the champion for the underdog. Nobody need suffer. She believes in the truth and what is right and fair. She doesn't consider the consequences. This often gets her into trouble. To the adults around her, she feels out of control and they have absolutely no clue how to handle her. They think she is a troublemaker but really, it's her way of protecting the people she loves dearly. Her loyalty knows no bounds.

I cannot stand *'Show Ruby'*. She's totally fake, with her jazz hands and all. It takes so much energy to be her. She can turn on the charm and be whatever you want her to be. She is my family's creation. She exists because they do. Our family is all about the image—the house, the photos, the parties and the good times. We put on a great act at The Hologram House to all the friends who come over after school and at the weekend. We're fooling them all. They all believe this is how we really are. If only they knew. I hope the smart ones can see through it and are too polite to say.

Sam and Gloria are really kind friends. They are a bit older than my parents. I see them as stand-in grandparents. They take care of us when my parents need a break. My Mum needs a break from me. She complains about me a lot and I don't like that. I want to overhear her talking about me and know that she is saying something kind. She seems to be so unhappy about everything. In the school holidays, we go and stay with Sam and Gloria by the seaside. Gloria is a homemaker. She bakes cakes and biscuits, sews and potters in the garden. She had once told me about the blue orbs that appeared when she took photographs of me and the girls playing in the garden. She claimed that the orbs were the energy of fairies or elemental spirits of the forest. Now I had met Nettie, I know for sure this is true! Gloria loves listening to my funny poems and is really interested in my drawings. She sees the detail in my artwork and is proud to show it to all her friends when they come over for tea. Sam loves to garden too, and he reads the newspaper a lot like my Dad.

I think the newspaper is my Dad's security blanket. Like a barrier that stops me from reaching him. I know that he really isn't listening. 'I ate a poo sandwich at school today, Dad!' 'Did you? Oh, that's lovely,' he would mumble without even lifting his head from the stupid newspaper. He carries it everywhere and spends most of his free time with it. He even falls asleep in it. I wonder if it's like my books are to me. A way to relax and zone out from the world. I know that when I'm in a book, I'm not really here. I want time out. I want quiet time away from people because it can get too noisy and intense. Especially, my Mum because she doesn't ever stop. She has the tenacity of a Wildheart. That must be where I get it from. You cannot say no to her. Well, you can, but just you wait and see what happens when you do. It's not pretty.

My Dad hides behind that newspaper and it's definitely a wall between us. I wish my Dad would sit with me and hold my hand while I read. Even if he reads over my shoulder and chews his tongue (which is by far his most annoying habit), I wouldn't mind. I wish he liked the same things that I like or at least pretended to be interested in me. It didn't have to be something for him, but something for 'us'. The closest thing I've found to that is watching the football with him on a Sunday afternoon. It's the most boring thing ever watching grown men in shorts kicking a ball all over the place, but if I stop talking, I can sometimes get a whole 90 minutes of snuggling into the sawdust smell that I love. And if I'm really smart, and learn the players' names, I can comment along on the game with him and cheer loudly when they score. I hate it but he seems to like that. He's happiest when I can meet him in his world. I don't think he can meet me in mine. Is that because I'm a girl and he's a boy?

I've seen him do that for my Mum though. He takes her shopping and to the theatre. He mows the lawn and cleans the cars and school shoes. He wants to make her happy which as I've already explained is an impossible job. I guess what with that, his work, and the garden—he really doesn't have any more spare time. I've seen him do that for my little sister too, but that's easier because she is sports mad just like him.

My Mum, on the other hand, doesn't hide between books and newspapers. She will get sick with stress or she gets caught up in being busy. You'll find her mostly standing in the kitchen wearing yellow rubber gloves ready to tackle her neverending list of chores. There are lots of jobs to do in our big house. When my Mum is really upset, I see her picking up fluff from the carpet. She doesn't stop until everything is perfectly done. She will whisk my unfinished drink away to be stacked into the dishwasher. She is a little firecracker too.

When I'm lost and miserable is when I feel least like any of the Rubys. I'm not Show Ruby, Resting, or Rageful Ruby. I'm just Nothing Ruby. I don't cry. I'm not angry. I'm all turned off and done in. I have nothing left to give. I am empty and lost. I don't know what will ever stop the emptiness. My parents try hard, but I make too many demands on them. I think I annoy both of them in my attempts to get their attention away from the newspaper and the chores. I've worked out that they do notice me when I get angry. Admittedly, it hurts to feel ignored, but I don't like to feel sad about it. I feel more powerful when I'm angry.

That's how I met Nettie, when I was having an angry outburst and had been sent to my room to think about what I had done.

'I knew you were a Wildheart the moment I heard your call.' said Nettie.

'I didn't call. You just showed up!' I argued.

'You have the cry of an angry bear and the heart of a teddy bear,' she leaned forward and put her hand on the top of my shoulder. We were sitting on the end of my bed which was rather crumpled from the swan diving and thrashing about. I'd landed head-first into my pillow muffling my angry cries and hammered my fists into the mattress. It felt good to pound away all that boiling fury.

'People can't tell you who you are. When they misunderstand you, naturally you are angry. Deep inside, you know who you are. You know the truth. People see what they want to see and what suits them.'

Nettie got up from the bed and started rummaging in her rucksack.

'What is a Wildheart?' I asked impatiently. My curiosity was getting the better of me.

'Well, what do you know?' she chuckled. 'You sure like to ask all the questions!'

'When you really know yourself, nobody can tell you who you are. They might have their experience of you, but that will depend on their view of life. It won't be about you.'

I scrunched up my nose. I didn't understand. Nettie stuck out her neck and gazed intensely into my eyes. She lowered her voice, 'I see you as you truly are. I have no filters. I don't care if you have dirty fingernails or bogies. I don't need you to be good, or well behaved. I don't see you as your homework or your school grades. I know in your heart you're full of love and kindness. I know you're a helper, but sometimes, it comes out a little wonky …' she trailed off to walk around behind me. I turned my head to follow her.

'I'm glad I'm not my school grades. I don't really like school. There's too much pressure and not a lot of fun,' I mumbled, worried that she might tell me off for bad mouthing school.

'Your honesty is refreshing, Ruby. People say they want honesty but when you give it to them, they're upset and you're the mean one for telling the truth. To tell the truth takes courage. And not everybody is prepared to face their truth. Wildhearts have courage by the bucket load.'

She went on, 'You're not what the teachers at school say you are. They only come to know a small part of you—the part that ticks boxes for their reports. You can't be put in a box. Look!' she insisted as she pushed me towards the mirror hanging on the nearby wall. 'Look at you!'

I briefly glanced towards the mirror and hung my head in shame. It was like being wronger than wrong. I didn't want to be seen in the mirror, I wanted to melt away. My freckly cheeks were flushed and blotchy from crying. My eyes were swollen, and I could feel my tummy clench.

'See yourself. Meet your own gaze,' she pleaded. 'You're a Wonderful Wildheart. Know yourself in full colour. Don't turn the colour down on your vibrant self so you fit in this black and white world.'

I lifted my head and winced at my reflection in the mirror.

'There's nothing to be afraid of. You're fine as you are,' she reassured me.

Nettle pulled out of her rucksack a neat roll of thick paper. Puzzled, I watched her wrestle with the curling paper, wondering how I could help. No sooner had she flattened out one end, smoothing the thick white paper on the floor, it would spring back again. It was so frustrating, but she remained unflustered. Without talking, I grabbed the other end and as she continued to flatten and smooth down hers, it finally stopped curling. She secured my end by placing her rucksack firmly on top of the rolled-out paper.

'Thank you! Now, write your question on the scroll,' she said handing me a large white feather. 'You do that a lot,' she said rolling her eyes. 'When you aren't sure, you pull a face.'

I stuck my tongue out and we giggled. Kneeling on the floor, I wrote in big letters in the middle of the page 'What is a Wildheart?' I put The Feather on the carpet next to me and sat back on my haunches.

I looked at Nettie. 'Now what?' I enquired.

Silence. I pulled a face.

Suddenly, The Feather sprang into action, scribbling furiously. As it filled up the page, the scroll grew longer and longer. *How on earth was Nettie going to get that back into her rucksack?* I wondered.

Wildhearts are deeply sensitive. Everything sticks like Velcro. The energy in the air and other people's feelings. We can walk into a room and pick up on the mood. This is a gift because as well as sensing the truth, we can also sense what isn't there or unsaid. Wildhearts know when people are lying. Their strong radars can detect when something feels off.

'It can get quite overwhelming when you feel like that,' Nettie acknowledged. 'You don't know what's you and what's other people.'

The Feather wiggled and scribbled,

Wildhearts can even sense what will happen before it does, or know what others want to say before they speak. Wildhearts just know, even when there's no proof except their strong belief that it is so. Sometimes they feel like they've been somewhere or met somebody before.

'That's déjà-vu,' Nettie chipped in.

Wildhearts have a razor-sharp awareness. They're super alert and notice the detail. It's like another sense. Some people call it intuition. In their hearts they carry great wisdom which is installed at birth like an in-built Google app. When Wildhearts learn how to allow and trust that inner wisdom, it automatically guides them. It's not to be messed with or to be feared. It's not to be controlled or contained. When you learn it and understand it, it's something you can use for good.

'Sound familiar, Ruby?' Nettie watched me deep in thought as I read the words unfolding on the page. I pulled another face. 'Have you got wind?' she teased.

Imagine the mind of a detective that adds up all the clues, and pieces the bits of the story together to solve the mystery. Deep thinking and forever curious, Wildhearts ask why and they want answers. Give a Wildheart a challenge and watch them get the job done. They don't hang about.

'I'm not so good at adding up, but I do irritate people with my constant chatter and questioning. I need things to make sense and I want to understand,' I reasoned.

Nettie nodded and smiled. 'The Soul Scroll holds the eternal Wildheart teachings,' she revealed. The intense energy of the words is mesmerising as the feathery, delicate, cotton-like threads flutter and dance above the page. 'These teachings can only be shared with those who truly understand,' she interrupted the moment.

Wildhearts have big hearts and care deeply. They're loyal and stick up for the underdog. You'd be glad to have them by your side. Their determination is steely and unbreakable. You cannot get a Wildheart to change their minds if they truly believe.

'I thought I was bad to be stubborn,' I let out a sigh.

'Not at all. You have to pick your battles,' Nettie challenged me. 'When it's something that you deeply care about, you stick to your principles.'

It was my turn to nod. I was hypnotised once again by The Feather swishing over the page.

Wildhearts are complicated with many layers. People are confused and misunderstand the opposing parts inside of them.

'It's like this—weightless, soft, and gentle.' Nettie pointed at The Feather which was taking a well-earned break. 'Then you discover an unstoppable energy and passion.' The Feather started up again.

Gentle and fierce. Caring and rageful.

Sensitive and tough. Creative and practical.

Innocent and wise. Flighty and steadfast.

Make believe and honest. Thoughtful and chatty.

Oh my! I think as I realised how naked I feel. The Feather picked up the pace. You could feel the urgency as the words poured out onto the paper.

I'm excited and relieved to learn all these new discoveries. 'I don't need to look in the mirror,' I exclaimed putting my hands on my cheeks. 'The Soul Scroll can see inside me!'

Wildhearts have strong morals and principles woven into their soul. Above all, they want to do the right thing. Their sensitivity allows them to put themselves in other people's shoes. Their empathic and loyal nature is what makes them great friends. They really do understand how other people feel. If at any time, they feel they can't trust you or you have crossed the line, they will be off.

People come to them when there's a problem. They want to make right the wrongs and live in peace and harmony.

'It sounds cheesy, but I have to say that with every single bit of my being, I strongly believe that bad can be turned into good. Don't you?' Nettie wondered aloud.

'I don't know.' I pulled another face.

'That's what being here is all about,' she continued. 'Learning, understanding, creating, and sharing. Rinse and repeat.'

Wildhearts want to break down old ways of being. They don't just make plans, they make plans happen. They are the change makers. They bring ideas to life and lead revolutions. Lots of Wildhearts have experienced immense sadness and loneliness. They want a better world for others and their pain is what fuels their desire for something more loving and less painful.

'I don't have a master plan,' I stressed.

'That's okay.' Nettie stepped in with her reassurance. Nothing fazes her.

'I'm not creative.' I insisted.

'Not true, Ruby! Creativity is when your heart and brain come together. It's when you have too much sensitivity and intelligence,' Nettie shot back.

Expect the unexpected. Take away the word 'normal'. Wildhearts work around the rules. They won't be hemmed in. They have crazy creativity that they use to solve problems and challenges. They have an amazing imagination which is limitless. Wildhearts flourish with responsibility. They are natural leaders and are comfortable taking charge. People are drawn to their energy.

Nothing will beat them. They get scared but they have the courage to do what they know they must do. They dare to tread a different path, and it's not always the easiest one.

'The path to The Wilderness isn't for people who do things by halves,' Nettie added.

'Is that where you're from?' I began to piece it all together like the super detective I now knew that I was. 'So, basically,' I summed up. 'We're called Wildhearts because we're creative change makers that lead from the heart with our fiery courage and steely determination.' Then I paused for dramatic effect. '… but we're also deeply sensitive and full of love.'

The Soul Scroll and its feathery friend swished backwards and forwards applauding in unison. Nettie threw her head back squealing with delight. 'Eeeeeeeee. That's my girl, Ruby! You're definitely one of us!'

CHAPTER 4

THE HOLOGRAM HOUSE OF HORRORS

I slept better that night than any of other times I had been sent to my room. Usually, it took ages to settle without a goodnight kiss which could have washed away the anger and brought an end to the drama. I hadn't felt as lonely because Nettie had been with me. Before she left, she handed me a daisy from her crown.

'Before you ask,' she had said, 'why don't you wait and see?' I wasn't very good at waiting for answers.

I had watched the scroll tightly curled itself around The Feather. Nettie somehow managed to push them firmly into her rucksack. Rather like watching my Dad shove a whole sausage in this mouth sideways. I noticed there was a big red 'W' sewn on one of the rucksack pockets, and I assumed Nettie must be a Wildheart too.

It felt easy to trust Nettie's judgement. I looked at the daisy in the palm of my hands, remembering The Soul Scroll. As I followed her instructions—to leave it under my pillow—I felt lighter knowing that I wasn't broken or bad. I was just me. If only I could convince my parents. I had to make them understand, so our family could be happy again. I felt excited as I drifted off to sleep.

I drew back the curtains and was met by a foggy morning. 'Brrrr!' I shivered and slipped back under the duvet. I sunk into deep thoughts which were switched on the minute I opened my eyes. The smell of warm cat breath wafted across my face and I was rudely interrupted by a loud purr in my left ear.

'Morning, Tom!' I said, half annoyed and half delighted to see him. I didn't like being on my own. Goodness knows I'd had enough practice, but there's nothing like the greeting of a furry friend to make you feel like yourself again. I am '*Restful Ruby*' when we're together.

'Life's not fair!' I blurted at Tom, parroting my parents' harsh reality. 'Except I don't believe that's true.'

His greenish-yellow eyes listened intently. 'I simply don't believe that life is that simple and rigid. It's not all one thing or the other. It's not black and white,' I debated, grateful that Tom had a better listening ability than either one of my parents.

'If it's black and white, one thing or the other, there's no intelligence. No learning, no discovering.'

Sometimes life is super unfair, I thought, remembering Annie and Poppy from school. Their families were being broken apart by Cancer and divorce. It was tragic that there wasn't an awful lot to console them. Perhaps only the promise of more joy. Joy waited patiently on the other side of their grief.

'So, Tom! I put it to you—could you appreciate one without the other? Could you know joy and excitement if you hadn't felt desperate sadness?'

'No, exactly,' I answered for him. He was too busy cleaning himself with his sandpapery tongue. I ran my hand across his soft, warm fur and as I reached his tail, he pushed his bottom in my face. I moved out of the way and continued with my freedom speech.

'Besides, Tom. Look at what lives between joy and sadness. It's not black and white—it's all the colours of the rainbow. To not live life in colour is to miss out on all the bits in between.'

Have you ever looked at a black and white picture and thought that a sprinkle of colour would bring it to life? Living in a drab colourless world wasn't truly being alive now, was it? I didn't have this black and white filter like my parents. My world stretched beyond the shades of grey and was a full kaleidoscope of bright colour. That's what made life deep and complex. Life was also uncertain. Only death was set in stone and even then, you didn't know when that would be. You might not know what tomorrow brings but you could show up and give it a go anyway.

'Does the black and white filter take away the bits we are unsure about, or is life meant to be exciting and not set in stone' I pondered. 'Is black and white safer and more comfortable? Is it less messy than feeling helpless and drowning in not knowing? Yes, Tom, I hear you, buddy,' I giggled, putting on my best Nettie voice. 'It limits our choices and shrinks confusion. The black and white rulebook says it can only be this way or that way. There is no room for anything new or different.

That is not allowed.' I did my best impression of an air stewardess, moving my hands to show the emergency exits to the left and right of me.

Tom purred louder as if he was cheering me on and I loved my listening friend even more.

'Can you imagine a black and white world without learning new things or being allowed to explore? How would we have discovered that the earth is round and salted caramel is a flavour of ice cream, after all?'

'Here's the thing,' I went all American and very serious, as I declared, 'Without understanding more, we are stuck. We feel alone. We fade away. Am I making any sense?' I asked Tom who was now clawing the pillow next to me.

My Dad wrongly assumed he knew what was right for me and would often say, 'You just want your own way!' That wasn't entirely true. I had more chance of getting some of my own way if I followed the strict, black and white rules, but even then, it usually went in their favour. This made me angry too. Truth be told, I was happier letting others have their way. That felt kinder and it was more important to be kind than right. Was it unreasonable to sometimes want things on my terms? How come they were forever on my Dad's?

I had considered the possibility that he actually wanted *his* own way because any other way was unknown to him, and therefore, it was scary and threatening. Another layer of uncertainty he wasn't prepared for, he didn't understand, and he didn't want to know about. Was it so hard for him to step into my shoes and appreciate my world, even though it was different from his? Neither of us had to be right or wrong, but we could both be 'different'. I guess it was.

It was more about being true to my feelings and my view of the world. Surely, two people could exist in the same family with different views of the world and not fall out? Did one person have to be right and the other wrong? Could you feel angry with somebody and still love them? Could you order pasta, the other person pizza, and still share a meal together? Was it possible that the sun and Moon could exist in the same sky without a fallout?

Of course it was, but in a black and white world where only one way is right and the other way is wrong, I was destined to spend every day of my existence feeling wretchedly wrong. I felt so ashamed of my 'wrongness' because it hurt me. To set myself free from this painful struggle, I constantly tried to prove my 'rightness'. My Dad called me a show-off. Was I to remain forever 'wrong' in his eyes or would he ever see the 'right' in me? I wanted life to be balanced, equal, and fair. I wished somebody would understand.

Life in The Hologram House was anything but that. It was an illusion. With magic, trickery, and sleight of hand, people saw something very different than what it really was. They believed the lie. They loved the firework shows, the elaborate Christmases, and fancy dinner parties. It was like a virtual reality game, where my parents were the rulers, creators, and winners. Like masters of projection, they beamed their righteous Hologram to the world that nothing was wrong here. Not with them anyway, just their children who are too much like hard work!

The Hologram House was attractive and appealing to many. My parents had so many friends and people who copied them. Jasmine, a girl in my class said she wanted to have a family like mine. I didn't know if I should be flattered or worried. It was a bit like taking a bite out of a big red apple expecting sweet juiciness, only to find mouldy maggots wriggling inside. On the outside everything is like in the movies—manicured gardens and finger nails. Polished expensive cars and holidays. Privately educated children who did their homework and got top grades. Exquisitely decorated rooms inhabited by well mannered, obedient children: clothes immaculate, not a hair out of place. There was no room for error, lateness, forgetfulness or laziness. Smile everybody!

Nobody saw the energy that went into keeping The Hologram alive. You couldn't imagine how exhausting it was to pretend and live a double life. Like a skilful puppeteer, my Mum had a hand in directing this great show. When the show was over and the front door was closed, nobody could hear the muffled screams on the inside. Nobody could feel the tension or the fear of the storm that raged chaos every day. Nobody could see the invisible controlling hand that lurked in the darkness and made us all play our parts so perfectly. Nobody could imagine what that was like. Nobody would believe it. How could they, when the masterful trickery did such a good job of hiding everything so perfectly?

That's how '*Show Ruby*' was born. I had to become a faker like them to survive it—, only from time to time when it was needed. I couldn't do it all the time. Only when the occasion demanded it. Do you know the story of the 'Emperor's New Clothes?'

There was an emperor who spent millions of pounds to have some new clothes made. They were magic clothes and could only be seen by wise people, but the tailors tricked him. The clothes are like The Hologram—they don't exist. The Emperor did not want to admit he could not see the clothes, because he does not want to appear rude or stupid. However, he is *very* stupid. Either that, or he is afraid to speak up and tell the truth. He is the only person who can see there are no clothes, so he wonders if he is going a little mad. I know how he feels.

I think when you say something over and over to yourself, it becomes the truth. You can convince your brain that the lie is the truth. It's easier to fall in line with what everybody else is thinking instead of going your own way.

'Just because somebody says it's the truth, doesn't mean that it is.' I reasoned. 'It can be scary to stand alone. It takes courage to tell the truth when you think people won't believe you,' I echoed Nettie's words to Tom. "Once, I was honest,' I confessed to Tom, saddened that I had let myself down. I had frozen over a part of my heart to keep The Hologram alive. I had almost given up what mattered most to me in the hope *they* would love and accept me. It hadn't worked and so, what was the point?

Luckily, there was a tiny bit of me that didn't quite want to believe in the lie. It was hard for a girl like me to lie. I had to cut off *some* of my feelings to pretend, but not all of them. I had lots of messy, ugly feelings which overshadowed The Hologram. They had a mind of their own and no matter how hard I tried, I couldn't stop them from leaking out. Every day, the battle in my head was between what I thought was the truth and what *they* were saying was the truth. Often, *they* would make me doubt myself, which was scary. I had started to distrust what I was thinking and feeling. As the doubt grew bigger, it took what was left of my confidence.

'Everybody wants The Hologram house so much, and I want to please my parents. I want to make them happy and proud. I want them to love me!' I sighed.

My Dad was wrong—it didn't feel very much like getting my own way. This wasn't my way at all.

Tom wrapped his tail around my head. 'Alright! Alright! I'll get your breakfast. You've been such a good listener.' I thanked him with a little kiss on top of his head. I had fallen for his feline charms and was feeling slightly defeated by these new revelations. I slowly got dressed for school. I hate wearing a uniform.

I tried hard to distract myself and think of something else as I spooned the brown jelly cat food into Tom's bowl. He curled in and out of my legs making a figure of eight with his tail around my woolly tights. I didn't fancy breakfast. I picked up my cheese and cucumber sandwiches from their home on the kitchen worktop. Mine were first in the line of carefully wrapped foil parcels neatly laid out in birth order and labelled with our names. Mine first, then Jemima, Jasmine (Jaz) and Nellie. They wouldn't make it to lunchtime today, I was already making a plan to eat them at playtime.

Jemima and I are at the same school as we are very close in age — only eighteen months apart. Sometimes, we end up getting told off together and both end up in our rooms. Although Jemima is much better at 'keeping her lip zipped' —another one of my Dad's gems. We have these really cool walkie-talkies that we use to chat to each to each other, but we have to be careful that we don't get caught. Jemima doesn't talk as much as me. When we were little, my Mum said that I used to talk for her. She's quite shy too and happy for me to take the lead. We take it in turns to be the big sister, but

I think Jemima is closer to Jaz and Nellie. We play together sometimes and we definitely spend a lot of time fighting. I guess all siblings do. We can be incredibly mean to one another one minute, then the next, we're snuggled up on the sofa watching movies and laughing our heads off. It's more changeable than the weather in The Hologram House!

I don't think any of them wanted to get too close to me, because I was the trouble maker. They worked hard to keep my parents happy, stay quiet and out of trouble. I was more fearless. Bring it on! We all baby Nellie! I secretly wish I was the youngest because Nellie gets heaps of hugs and kisses. Everybody adores her and likes to pick her up. I guess it's because she is dinky like a doll. She really doesn't seem to mind that much. She is more agreeable than me! I really can't deny that she is super cute. I would trade places with Nellie in a heartbeat. I'd gladly give up my bossy-being- in-charge-big-sis role for that kind of love and affection. On a Sunday morning, Jemima and I go and drag Nellie out of her cot, so my parents can sleep in. We literally have to drag her over the bars because we're not quite tall enough to reach in and scoop her up like they do. We take real pride in being the big sisters and enjoy taking care of her.

Everybody confuses Jaz and me because, at a glance, we look pretty similar. Jaz lets me do her hair and make-up. She makes a much better model than my dolls. She also loves to dance too. She's much better than me, she can even sit in the splits!

I shut the front door behind me. As soon as I was out of sight, I loosened my tie. I wanted to breathe in the crisp morning air from the cosy warmth of my winter coat. I disappeared into the fog and headed off in the direction of school. It took me about 20 minutes to get there. Jasmine and I usually walked together, but she was going on her bike today. Some days I would cycle but the mudguard on my bike needed fixing again, so today I was on foot. I made my way through the mist. I looked down to watch my step. When I looked up again, a white feather dropped from the sky and floated past my nose to the ground. I looked up expecting to see a bird, but I couldn't see very far ahead. I cut down the Bumpy Lane and began thinking about The Soul Scroll and The Feather. My earlier disappointment was outshone by the more exciting revelations of being a Wildheart. The other stuff could keep. It wasn't like I was going to be able to do anything about it any time soon.

'I wonder if there are more of us!' I smiled.

Mentally reciting the register in my head, I thought about the bravest children in my class. Annie's Grandma was dying. Poppy's Mum and Dad were splitting up. Callum was dyslexic. He could be a Wildheart because he could get very angry too. It suddenly dawned on me that courage doesn't have to be loud. Who knows how much strength it takes other people to go about their lives? I thought about Mrs Barnes, my form tutor and wondered if she ever got nervous about speaking in front of the class. I certainly did. I decided to make today at school fun. I would see how many Wildheart qualities I could spot in my classmates. I wished I didn't have to hide mine so much, but they seemed to be the source of all my troubles, so best I didn't show off.

At 3.30 pm the school bell rang and my cheeks hurt from smiling so much. 'You're very happy today, Ruby,' Mrs Barnes remarked. I put my books and pencils away in my desk and started to line up by the classroom door ready to be dismissed.

I was really good at pretending to be happy but today my smiles felt real. They had shone straight from my heart and lit up the whole of my freckly face. I had given extra smiles to Annie and Poppy. Smiles were contagious and the girls showed their appreciation by smiling back at me too. I was proud that my smiles were cheerleaders, willing the girls on for being so brave. I could see Callum didn't enjoy our last lesson. It was like Nettie had said, I could feel his frustration and sadness from across the room. I had caught it and now I felt wonky. I watched him score out words in his book and drop his shoulders with heavy sighs. I tried to lean over to see if I could help, but Mrs Barnes caught me with a look that said, 'Don't do that!' I thought better of it and sat back in my chair, annoyed that she wasn't noticing Callum's struggle.

Walking home, I thought about what I could have said to Mrs Barnes. I liked to talk to myself and pretend role play when I was alone. It got the words off my chest. 'Couldn't you see Callum was struggling?' I mustered up all the courage in my Wild Heart. 'If only teachers would listen more. If only adults would remember how it feels to be learning. We don't want you to do anything, just listen and show us that you understand,' I said, sounding like my Mum's 'Get here now!' voice.

Why was this so hard for adults? I was starting to realise that feeling understood and knowing you're not wrong for being different was what made it great to be a Wildheart. If you're not wrong, you cannot get the blame, can you? That would make such a nice change.

When I got home, I rushed past my Mum who was standing at the kitchen sink peeling potatoes. As I headed for the playroom to join the girls, she piped up, 'Don't start getting everything out now. Your dinner will be ready soon.'

My Mum's clock was different to the rest of the world. Like she was in a different time zone, the clock ticked on her terms. 'Soon' could mean minutes or it could mean hours. You weren't to question it even if you were hungry. The only thing was, I didn't have hours to wait, I wanted to go and meet Nettie. I stopped in my tracks. I was still grumpy after last night, but the promise of seeing Nettie again helped me to feel less so.

'Did you hear me, Ruby?' her voice sharpened. I irritated her and she irritated me.

'Yup' with the emphasis on the 'P', I puffed out my cheeks. I didn't mean for that to come out so sassy. I clenched my bottom cheeks and jaw hoping she didn't notice. I held my breath waiting for her response. It was tense because you never knew which way it was going to go.

'Can you lay the table, darling? she asked. The sugary sweet tone hung in the air. Nope, she hadn't felt the sass. It was mind-boggling how she flip-flopped from one mood to another. It was like the Guess Who of Mums. You didn't know which one you were going to get. I made it my job to handle Mum, because I decided as the eldest it was down to me to step up. Besides, I gave as good as I got and my Mum seemed to like that. The others left me to it.

I took the mats and cutlery out of the drawer and laid them on the kitchen table. I went to the cupboard hunting for the salt and pepper. As I took them back to the table to complete my task, it hit me from the side. Like it had floated from the sink from where she was standing. I could feel her mood. Without looking up from the chopping board, she moaned about my Dad. She quickly and skillfully cut each potato into four pieces and plopped them into boiling water. The more she worked herself up into a frenzy, the quicker she chopped and plopped. I zoned out. I liked disappearing into my head when the atmosphere became a little too choppy.

I had considered testing the waters to see if she would buy the story about my Wildheart spirit, but something stopped me. It didn't feel like the right time. I wanted to keep it to myself. It was like I had something they couldn't take away. It made me feel less bad and slightly more powerful.

We don't have secrets in our house. 'Liars always get found out!' my Mum would say. Ironic as she was the biggest liar of all. During dinner I started to feel bad that I was holding in something I should have shared with her. The guilt made it hard for me to eat. The thick, buttery mash lodged at the back of my throat and I wondered if I really was as bad as they said I was after all.

I forced it all down and then helped clear the table. The rules were if your plate made it to the sink, then it could make it into the dishwasher which was inches away. If your plate made it to the sink and didn't make it into the dishwasher, well that was another story entirely. As I said—it could go one of two ways. They were the unwritten rules of The Hologram House. It was black or white. Right or wrong. On a good day, she'd do it for you and tell you not to worry. She'd wave you off into the playroom to watch your favourite TV programme. On a bad day, you could wind up in your bedroom with the immortal words: ‘Wait until your father gets home!’ hanging over your head. Today, I had no time to waste, so my plate made it to the dishwasher, and I escaped to my room.

I had hidden the daisy in my slippers which lived at the end of my bed. I still wasn’t sure what the daisy was for, but I climbed up onto the window with it and waited. I looked down at the patio and then out way beyond the fir trees where Snowy lived. ‘Where is she?’ I said to myself impatiently.

Nettie was nowhere to be seen. Forever hopeful and loyal, I took up my spot on the windowsill and waited for her return.

CHAPTER 5

THE WILD, WILD WILDERNESS

I wasn't very good at waiting, so this was good practice. I have to admit it did feel very strange racing to my room without being sent there as a punishment.

'Let's get you out of here,' whispered a voice from behind the curtain.

I smiled. There she was all flowery and curly, her rucksack bobbed behind her and her little silver sandals shimmered around her toes. There was no sign of the Soul Scroll and I wondered what was in store for me today.

'Hurry, we haven't got much time before it gets dark,' she calmly announced.

Swiftly, she pushed her small fingers into the crown resting on her head. I watched her carefully pluck another daisy from amongst the mass of dark curls that fell over her ears and shoulders. As she handed it to me, I noticed that the middle of it was not yellow, but deep purple.

'Here. Take this moonflower in both hands and hold it in front of your heart,' she instructed. 'Your heart is where your strength lives. No faces! Open your heart and feel, Ruby.'

I noticed the petals began glowing violet and as I drew the flower across my heart, they shivered. A warm rush of calm slowly filled my body. I listened carefully to Nettie's guidance. 'Now, close your eyes and breathe. This activates your heart energy,' she paused. 'No faces. Hold still, Ruby.'

My tummy was flipping between scared and excited. I closed my eyes and waited. Nothing happened. I stood still with my eyes shut tight, but desperately wanting to peek. After a while, my brain started to worry if my parents were going to miss me. Visions of them sending out search parties into our street filled my head. There were posters of my face stuck to every lamp post. People seemed genuinely concerned as to my whereabouts.

Don't be ridiculous! They like it when you're in your room—it gives them peace and quiet. They won't even know that you're gone, I reassured myself.

'Open your eyes,' Nettie interrupted my fantasy moment. I opened my eyes and found myself in complete darkness. 'I can't see,' I complained. The moonflower must have heard me as its ultraviolet rays lit up.

Is it a cave or a tunnel? It could be a tunnel, I pondered. My detective mind kicked in and wanted to work it all out.

'Where are we?' I felt afraid. I couldn't see Nettie and I could no longer feel her calming energy beside me.

Nothing. My fear of the dark had kicked in. When I can't sleep, I lie in my bed and see strange and scary shapes in the shadows. I know they are not real, but they feel sinister. I was not made for darkness. I started to breathe quickly. Short little bursts of air came out of my mouth as if I was blowing out birthday candles. My chest rapidly rose up and down with each pant. I put my hand on my chest to steady my breathing.

'Nettie!' I hollered into nothingness. 'Where are you?' I felt desperate and panicky. My breathing rushed louder and louder in my ears. Gripping fear zapped through my chest. I put my other hand on my heart and pressed down. My tummy felt tense and knotted. I picked up the pace and started to run, scrambling to get away from all these uncomfortable feelings. I didn't know where I was going. I could barely see. The violet light from the moonflower flickered.

'Noooo,' I cried out. 'Please don't turn out the light. Please! Please don't leave me here in the darkness by myself. I can't ...' my voice trailed off as I turned my head from side to side, unable to see a thing. The light had gone out. Trying to block out the terror of being lost and alone in the dark, I had an idea. I held the moonflower in both my hands, placed them over my heart and closed my eyes. As I breathed in, I felt the cool air inside my nose and warm calm flood my body.

A few more breaths and my eyes started to adjust to the darkness. I seemed to be inside an archway. The walls looked like they were made of wood. It smelt earthy like Snowy's shed, which funnily enough felt familiar and comforting in the darkness. It was as if Snowy could have been close by if I thought long and hard about it. I put my hand out and was surprised to feel the walls covered in big bumpy ridges. My brain that was now free from panic had the space to think and I was much more relaxed. I had worked it out—it was bark! My body melted slightly with relief as I realised I was inside a gigantic tree trunk. Somehow, giving my brain a job to do eased the panic and helped me regain a sense of calm. The air breezed through my lungs again—slower and steady—without much help from me.

The moonflower glowed brightly again, and in the distance I heard Nettie. Her laughter filled the dark hollow and evaporated my fear. Her voice grew louder and was reassuring. Without a moment to lose, I followed the echoing giggles, curious to know where they would lead. I had tumbled out of the gigantic tree trunk and onto the grass beneath me.

'Welcome to my home!' said Nettie, still laughing, her arms sweeping in a big 'ta-da' moment. I could feel the pride and happiness as she pointed to a sign that said, 'The Wilderness'.

I popped the moonflower in my pocket. When I felt unsure, I held onto things just in case I needed them again. Who knows when that might come in handy? I was astounded by the natural beauty that surrounded me. I stood captivated by the view, rich and colourful, like jumping into a freshly painted picture. I stood completely still to take it all in. Forget-me-nots, pansies and bluebells danced in front of lush green hills. They rolled on for miles to meet the blue sky in the distance. A white butterfly hovered over the tall grasses growing around the flowers. It couldn't seem to decide where to land. Finally, it settled on the pink petals of a Magnolia tree. I much preferred the wildflowers haphazardly strewn in colourful clumps instead of the orderly flowerbeds in our garden. They seemed happier growing on their schedule and relished the freedom to grow anywhere they pleased!

'Sam and Gloria would love it here,' I observed. I momentarily thought about home. I missed it. Was it possible to miss something you had mixed feelings for? Maybe it was the familiarly of what I knew. There was no guessing or not knowing. I wanted Tom, my bed, slippers, my books, and the familiar chaos.

'Where did you get to? We've been waiting for you,' Nettie softly enquired.

'Where did *you* get to?' I argued over the noise. It was hard to be heard over the fun and laughter. Children's spirits ran carefree as each one became lost in play. They were having the time of their lives. Some of them were enjoying pony rides, and others were picking fresh vegetables to feed rabbits. In the leafy green vegetable patch, I spied sweet yellow corn and juicy red tomatoes. I was relieved to see that there were no Brussel sprouts. I hate those little balls of poo. It wasn't unlike the vegetable patch at the top of our garden—potatoes, courgettes, and orange pumpkins that will be ready for carving at Halloween. The Wilderness was a blend of all seasons. Tall sunflowers reached up towards the sky, autumn leaves and acorns carpeted the ground, and all around was the scent of fresh herbs. My mouth watered as I could almost taste the sweet and peppery basil. I instantly thouhght of silky pesto pasta topped with strong cheese.

From the fairy-light covered bandstand, a small choir belted out a rather uplifting number. They swayed and clapped in time to the music. It was one of those rousing key changes that feel like the sound of renewed hope after a bad day. I loved it—you just sensed it was all going to turn out fine. The children were enchanted by the music too and their joy was contagious. They happily danced and sang, letting the music infuse their little bodies. Nettie was patiently waiting on standby for her turn to talk. The song ended and I felt a twang of disappointment. I had just begun to find my dancing feet and tap in time to the rhythm.

'You passed the test!' interrupted a little boy who was sat by the pond, fishing.

'What test?' I pulled a face. I thought about the tests at school that turn me into wobbly jelly. My tummy growled as if it remembered too. 'Too many chances to get it wrong!' it grumbled.

'You found your way through the darkness. You listened and you found your way,' the boy explained.

I walked over to the pond so I could hear him better. As I got closer I noticed that his ears were pointy at the ends and he was wearing a t-shirt with the same 'W' that I had seen on Nettie's rucksack. Next to the 'W' on the front it said 'Strong Belief ~ Wild Heart' in big bold letters.

'This is where all the Wildhearts belong. Look at them all,' gushed Nettie. 'So free! They can just be who they are. These children have decided to cross over and live here with us. Their bodies on earth are replaced with new souls – we call them 'Swapsies'. Their family and friends don't suspect a thing, because they look exactly the same. It's just their soul that has been switched. Some children learn lots while they are here and we prepare them so they can return home happier and calmer than when they first arrived.

'Did you leave me on purpose?' I snapped at Nettie, my cheeks turned red with anger.

'Are you cross with me, Ruby?' she reached out her hand and tried to grab mine. I snatched it back and stuffed my hands in the pockets of my school uniform. The children fell silent and began to walk away. One by one over the hills they went, leaving me and my anger to battle it out. *You're such an idiot! Look, they're all leaving, and you are the one who is frightening them away*, said the voice in my head.

I directed my anger at Nettie, 'That was mean to not tell me you were leaving. I was all alone back there in the dark.' I pointed to the tree behind me with my thumb like a hitchhiker. 'I hate it! I hate this!' I waved my hand at The Wilderness. 'There is no such place that will let you be who you are. Nobody will let me be who I am. Being me drives everybody away! You're just like all the others.' I shouted. 'You pretend to understand but you haven't got a clue. You're not listening. You don't even know me!' I kicked the acorns with my trainers and drew a breath to press on with my rant.

I was distracted by Nettie's attempt to reach my hand again. She smiled and said, 'You're right, Ruby, I don't know you. I thought I did,' she confessed keeping her tone light. ‘If I thought for one moment you would be *that* scared—and believe me I can see how scared you are right now—I would have stayed with you.’ Her eyes met mine and I could see that she meant it.

It felt so odd being angry with an adult who didn’t want to shut me down or make me wrong. Nettie didn’t want to banish me back into the dark tree trunk and make me think about what I had done. She didn’t want to abandon me, but instead, she listened. She tried hard to understand. I knew she was really trying because that’s how hard I try to understand my Mum. I could see all this good in her and yet I wasn’t able to stop myself.

I’m *not* scared, I’m fuming!’ I insisted on staying in the fight. I refused to let go of my anger. It felt right and strong. Besides, Nettie had shown me that she couldn’t be trusted. I was drifting off into my head again, when a voice said, *she is trying to be kind. Look! She wants to stay here and understand. She isn’t raising her voice. She won’t hurt you.* But I wasn’t ready to listen to my voice of reason.

‘Maybe I brought you here too soon,’ Nettie explained, ‘I was sure that you were ready. I’m sorry,’ she said. ‘I should have waited a bit longer. I think we need to take our time. Go slow. What do you think, Ruby?'

Hearing her say my name in such a calm, kind tone, softened my anger, and I let her take my hand.

'I misread things. It was totally my mistake. I can see why you would not trust me,' she went on. Her compassionate words taking down my angry wall.

'You made me take a test without telling me!' I started to cry now. She had soothed and dissolved my anger easily. It was far quicker than the day long stand offs in The Hologram House. My parents' approach couldn't be more different to Nettie's bomb disposal squad. She had skillfully gotten under my anger to my fear, whereas my parents usually added more petrol to the flames and left me to it.

'I thought we were going on a fun adventure. I don't even know where I am. I trusted you. I could have failed. I wasn't prepared. Why would you do that?' my brain had kicked in searching for answers again.

'I want to understand, Ruby, if you'll let me. I thought that if I told you there was a test, you wouldn't come.' She stood next to me and put her hand on the small of my back. 'I wouldn't set you up to fail. I want the best for you. I wanted you to see all of this,' she reasoned.

'You don't understand! If you don't get it right, you're bad. I'm sick of being bad.' I sobbed. 'Even when I'm good, it's not quite enough. I can't win.'

'You don't need to win. It's a ridiculously impossible game that's not worth playing.' Nettie moved her hand to the back of my head. 'There, there, Ruby', she whispered. 'Let all those tears out.' I felt safe again as she stroked my hair. It made me realise that my Mum and I didn't have much physical closeness, except when she wanted a hug. It wasn't surprising as I spent a lot of time pushing her away with my anger. Have you ever tried to hug an angry person? While I lay with my head on Nettie's chest, I pictured my Mum yanking my sister's knotty hair on days when we were late for school and everybody was tired and grumpy. Sometimes I was relieved I had short hair because I could style it myself and wouldn't get any of the angry ponytail treatment.

I stopped crying and Nettie handed me a tissue. Usually, when I flew off the handle it was a nighttime of stomping, door slamming, angry snotty tears, and not being able to sleep.

'Now! Can you forgive me? I have something you will really love. When it gets too much, simply say, 'STOP!' or something that warns me that the anger is coming. Then I can help you with that. I want to help you. To feel our fear and face it takes courage.'

'You passed the second test!' came a voice from the pond. The fisher boy with pointy ears punched the air and said, 'What a triumph! How good do you feel?'

'He's right,' Nettie agreed. 'You faced the darkness and it was painful, but it did not kill you. You found your way here and you were brave in spite of your fear. Then you faced your own angry darkness and it was upsetting, but it did not kill you. Nor did it upset or kill anybody else.'

'I noticed that all the children disappeared when I started to get angry,' I felt ashamed as I remembered them all running for the hills to get away from me.

'They had to go and have their tea,' Nettie laughed. 'Do you really think you have the power to make hundreds of children disappear? Firstly, you can't make anybody do anything they don't want to. And secondly, I don't find you scary one little bit.

I think you're actually very sweet. You're just misunderstood.'

How can she be so kind to me when I dared argue with her and say how I feel? I thought.

I took stock of the miracle that had occurred. Two big fears that ruled my little world had shrunk. I'd given them way too much power and all because I didn't know what else to do. It was nice to be shown there was another way. Nettie knew what was happening in my body. She knew that my anger was covering up my scareds, and that it was better to try and understand myself than to fear what I did not know. I've been terrified of the dark for as long as I can remember, and my temper had not yet been tamed. Instead it was sent away and shut down. It has all been possible with Nettie by my side. She had this overwhelming desire to understand me above anything else. With her, there was no right or wrong. No threat of a punishment and no 'Do as you're told!' She stayed calm and listened. In the silence, I was able to work it out for myself. I felt safe when I knew she was on my side. As if she could read my mind, Nettie's voice interrupted my thoughts, 'The light in your heart, Ruby, is stronger than any darkness. I have chosen to be the person to catch you when you fall and to help you feel safe. I do that because I want to and because I care. You're so easy to love and care for.'

CHAPTER 6

THE NOOK

‘Let’s take a moment,’ Nettie headed towards the tree tunnel that had brought me here. I flinched as I remembered fumbling in the darkness unable to breathe. Nettie walked around the front of the tree’s knobbly old body. We reached the hollow entrance. It reminded me of sitting in the dentist’s chair with my mouth wide open. I hate the dentist—the nasty vibrating drill shook my whole body. I didn’t have a very high pain threshold. ‘Stop making a fuss! You’ll be okay!’ they would tell me. At the other end, the big trunk forked off into tangled brambles. I couldn’t see where this other branch went, but peeping out from the masses of prickly shrubs, was a blue door. Nettie pushed it open.

We entered what looked like an underground cavern. I later discovered it was more fondly known as 'The Nook'. This was what Nettie called home. It was the very antithesis of my pristine white fitted wardrobes and perfect pastel bedroom. For a start, there were so many cobwebs. I winced picturing my Mum's sour face. She wouldn't have approved or allowed it to get so dusty. Over in one corner was a battered metal sink, a bit like the one at the end of the garden where my Dad grows mint. Above the sink was a shelf of wonkily piled pots and pans that looked like they might topple over. A red kettle hung over a log fire which was built into the mossy walls. It was small and cosy, the heat of the fire beefed up that familiar garden smell of Snowy's shed. Only it was mingled with the strong petal perfume of the moonflowers. Their purple glow lit up the room. Tiny twinkly fairy lights hung over pictures and tapestries that covered the walls.

I liked it. It was cosier than my bedroom. Things were haphazardly placed but were easy to see. They weren't neatly confined to dedicated 'homes' where they must be put back after use. God forbid anybody who didn't replace the toilet roll when they'd used the last sheet. Any bathroom behaviour was distinctly monitored. I often neglected hand washing, toilet flushing and toilet roll replacing because I was more intent on avoiding the man that lived in the toilet. He terrified me, and so my visits to the bathroom were rushed and frantic.

Nettie pointed at a bench carved into the wall. 'Sit yourself down!' she invited. She patted a big padded cushion. It was like the flowery ones that covered the toy boxes in my playroom. Big foam rectangles to protect your bottom from the cold hardwood. I made myself comfortable and Nettie went about fixing us a drink.

'All that emotional energy takes it out of you—time to refuel,' she said. 'Water okay?' I nodded. She handed me a glass. I hadn't realised how thirsty I was and eagerly guzzled it down. I carefully listened to Nettie's wise words. 'It's important to take care of your body,' she said. Her tone was one of concern and not like the fearful lecturing voice my parents used to get me to eat more greens. It was also less scathing than the one which banned me from having pudding because I hadn't eaten my greens.

'I think we need to be kinder to our bodies and not take them for granted. We expect them to do so much—learn, play, read, write, dance, and we want them to look nice, but we don't rest them properly and we don't put the right things in them,' she said.

I blushed, thinking about the chocolate stashed in the back of my wardrobe. I saved it up from Easter, so I had something to eat when I was stuck in my room. Well, I'm not really stuck. There's no lock on the door, but something tells me it's not safe to come out until *they* say I can. I'm too embarrassed to tell Nettie about the chocolate eggs. I also don't want her to know that I ask for a chicken leg when we have our roast dinner on Sunday so I can hide my sprouts under the crispy skin and still manage to score some apple pie and ice cream. My Mum is an excellent cook and she makes the best desserts ever.

'I love sugary treats,' I enthused. 'They make me happy.'

It was Nettie's turn to pull a face.

'For somebody who is very truthful you've just told yourself a big fib,' she giggled. 'How can something that poisons you, make you happy?'

'It's *not* poisonous. Salted caramel is the best ice cream ever invented.' I argued.

'How do you feel after your treats?' she asked. 'Go inside and scan your body. Tell me what it feels like after you've been treating yourself to sugar.'

I scratched my head. I hadn't really considered it until now. I squirmed, wondering how to work this one out.

'Well ... I guess I feel urrrm ... I feel ... full of energy. Yes, I feel buzzy for a bit. Then, I'm ratty and tired. My tummy sticks out and I have to undo the button on my jeans. I'm thirsty and my teeth are squeaky.' I finished.

'Squeaky mouse!' she joked in a high-pitched voice. 'So, what part of that feels good?' she challenged me with a cheeky grin.

'I don't know. It feels good to have a treat.' I was confused.

'What's good about it? I want to believe you, Ruby. Can you tell me *one* good thing?' I loved it that Nettie was willing me to be right and to talk so openly. I was really enjoying our debate and didn't feel angry at all.

'We get treats when we are good. If I have a treat, I'm not bad anymore.' I gasped realising what I had just said.

'You're not good or bad. You're Ruby. How can anybody decide that about you based on how you behave? Sometimes your behaviour may be what others don't want to see, but you're still learning. During the course of the day, we don't stay the same. From moment to moment, we can change depending on how we feel. So, we're not one thing or the other. Do you think treats are helpful? Do treats tell you who you are and how you feel?' She asked.

She wasn't waiting for my answer, because I'm vigorously nodding my head up and down like a yo-yo. I couldn't agree more.

'Only you know who you are and how you feel, Ruby. What makes you feel good? I saw you tapping your toes back there.' she signalled with her head in the direction of the bandstand.

'Yeah, I love dancing,' I said sheepishly. 'Music feels really good.'

'It sure does,' she agreed. 'The choir in the bandstand sing the sweetest songs. Music has a universal energy just like your heart energy,' she said. 'It can be electrifying and energising. It can also be sad and sorrowful as if it understands.'

'Is this where you sleep?' I'm distracted by all the new things in the room, I pointed to a comfy bed strewn with pillows and blankets in the opposite corner of the room. Nettie nodded.

'I'm a bit like you. I don't get much sleep.' Her kind eyes letting me know that she had listened and understood. 'So I read. Here, let me show you something.' She walked across the room and brushed her hand over one of the moonflowers shining brightly from behind her headboard. I jumped as the bed flipped backwards and disappeared into the wall.

I hadn't expected that. 'Wooooooow! That's awesome!' I shrieked. She sensed my fear again. 'You're safe here, Ruby. Come and see!' She beckoned me over to where she was standing.

We both stood where the bed had been and looked down. In its place was a winding staircase that went deep into the ground. 'It's really dark down there.' Nettie was worried that I was going to get scared like before. I retrieved the moonflower from my pocket and held it in my hands.

'It's okay, I know what to do. I'm ready, let's do this!' My fear was still there, but it was more a faint whisper than a loud roar. My curiosity had gotten the better of me and I couldn't wait to venture into the darkness.

Nettie and I were in perfect sync, smiling as we placed our hands over our hearts, closed our eyes and inhaled. Our heart energy lit our moonflower torches and we began our descent into the deepest darkest depths of the earth. I felt the tension in the air, just like I had before when I had made my way through the tree trunk tunnel alone. This time my breath didn't falter. With each step of the staircase, I felt more and more excited about what I might discover.

At the foot of the staircase, Nettie clapped her hands, 'Ra-ta-ta!'

Suddenly, the whole place was aglow with ultraviolet beams. Amongst the moonflowers was the biggest library I had ever seen. From floor to ceiling, were thousands of thick, heavy books, their delicate pages protected by rigid covers. Only a bookworm like me could swoon at this magnificent sight and feel nourished by their delicious aroma.

Now that did feel good, I thought. *Was it better than sugary treats? Maybe it was*! I begrudgingly admitted.

'This is the Life Library! The place where life stories are told, lessons are learnt, and wishes are granted!' Nettie proudly introduced me to dusty shelves of wisdom. I could see a long ladder leaning against the books nearby. The shelves were twice as tall as me. I could see that Nettie wasn't going to need the ladder—she had wings. In the middle of the room sat a long wooden table. Books were tumbling onto it and stacking themselves into two distinct piles. Fascinated by the hive of activity, I watched another book shoot onto the table. The Soul Scroll and The Feather went about their work, sorting the books into their correct piles.

'Busy little bees! It must be a New Moon,' Nettie remarked, and I noticed that one pile of books was significantly taller than the other. 'When there is a big, round Moon face in the sky, we call that a Full Moon. It marks the end of the Moon's cycle so it's a time for endings, goodbyes, and getting stuff done. At this time, lots of Wildhearts are letting go of and making space for new things to come in. After fourteen days, a New Moon cycle begins, and the Moon is invisible to the earth. It marks new beginnings, a symbol of fresh starts. This is when all the Wildhearts make their wishes. The first pile, the Gold Books, are for lessons learnt. Then the really tall tower of rainbow coloured books, they're all the wishes.'

I mentally note, *Gold Books: lessons learnt. Full Moon. Endings. Rainbow Books: wishes. New Moon. Beginnings.*

Nettie continued to explain, her eyes wide with excitement. 'Every time we feel a Wildheart is in trouble, we see how we can best help them. We came to you when we heard your angry cries. We tuned into the heart energy and it led us to you. In life, there are certain people we meet or certain events that need to happen to teach us valuable lessons. These lessons help us to grow and become the person we're meant to be. Even your family, Rubes—you were born into that family so you could learn some important life lessons. Everything happens for a reason.'

'I often thought it was the wrong family for me, but I didn't want to be mean to them, 'cos ... you know,' my voice faded, '... they're family after all.'

'Well, you have 2 weeks! By the time the Full Moon comes around again, I have a sneaky suspicion you will have lots of lessons to put in your Gold Book, and you can decide then.'

'Decide what?!' I pulled a face, my eyes wide with shock.

'You can decide if you want to do Swapsies,' she said as if it was no big deal.

'That sounds weird!' I said, unsure if Swapsies was really a thing. Mind you, fairy wings, moonflowers and magic had only been a figment of my imagination up until this point.

From deep in the underground cosiness of Nettie's home, I now realised why certain things were happening and had happened to me. 'Once you've learnt the lesson, it goes in a Gold Book and our two friends here file it away for safe keeping.' Nettie pointed to the Soul Scroll and The Feather who were caught up in their work.

'Like a school report of catastrophes,' I joked.

'We like to call them upgrades. When you upgrade, your whole being expands—your mind, your heart and your soul. Your heart energy increases and you feel better. Even though some of the lessons are tough and they generate big, scary feelings, they are good for you.'

'Like sprouts!' I cried.

Nettie laughs. 'Yes, like sprouts,' she confirmed. She continued, 'This is how The Soul Scroll and The Feather get inspired. They are powered by heart energy. They don't see this as work because their heart energy is magnified by helping other Wildhearts. It's what they came here to do.'

'What, you mean that heart energy is what makes this happen?'

Nettie nodded. 'Heart energy is the invisible force of the universe that lives in all of us. It's freely given. You don't need to earn it or do anything to access it except be open to it. Not everybody can access their heart energy.'

'What, not even if they put their hand over their heart with a moonflower like we do?' I asked.

'No, because people who are shallow, shut down, and rigid ... these people are afraid of living fully. Living a colourful life takes courage.'

'I was afraid in the tunnel but even when the moonflower flickered, the heart energy still came through,' I recalled.

'A child's wonderment and curiosity for life are huge. Lots of grown-ups lose that, but some of them are still searching. All the time you're searching and learning, you're open to an upgrade. Some grown-ups get caught up in the seriousness of daily life. When life becomes hard work it's like being on one of those running thingies at the gym, knee deep in peanut butter. They forget who they are and try to be like other people. They want to fit in. They don't question things or want to go against the grain. They forget about play and fun. They work, work, work to earn money because they think it will make them happy. They search for happiness in things that cannot give it to them. They feel disappointed and tired. They stop having desires and stop listening to their feelings. They switch off to learning lessons. They feel rubbish but still they continue to struggle.'

I think of my Mum standing at the sink, her yellow rubber-gloved hands in soapy water and my Dad getting up at silly o'clock to work at the shop. 'But without money, we can't go on holiday. When we're on holiday, my parents are really happy,' I said thinking aloud.

'Heart energy is the purest form of happiness and it's everlasting. It doesn't need holidays or sugary treats to feel good. It just is.'

I felt upset thinking about my parents in that way, so I changed the subject. 'Do I have a Gold Book?' I hesitated. I was worried that it may be a record of all my badness. That's not something I want to be put in writing. It could be used against me at any time.

'Oh, don't worry about that right now.' Nettie said. The Soul Scroll winked at me from the top of the ladder. 'The Soul Scroll can help us sift out the important bits. Believe me, you really don't want to spend hours reading all the Gold Books. It will knock you sideways. Wildhearts are super sensitive and deeply affected by what happens to other people and what goes on in the world. I need to teach you how to protect yourself. Besides, they're private, Ruby, and reading them is not a good use of your time. You have your own lessons to focus on. Your energy is better spent focusing on those.'

I moved from foot to foot and looked around for somewhere to sit. I ended up resting on a rung of the ladder. I leaned against the gold frame thinking how much I liked Nettie's sass. She was all fired up and spoke with her hands. She was usually so calm and serene, but this was clearly something that mattered to her and lit her up like a moonflower.

'The bigger the lesson, the greater the gift.' Nettie wagged her finger into the air. 'How do you think the coastline is made? When you're on the beach paddling your toes in the water, what is wearing away the stones, the rocks into soft fine sand?'

'So, lessons are like the sea, they shape us into the best version of ourselves?' I answered feeling quite smug. I wouldn't have risked answering if there was any risk of getting it wrong. This is what stole my voice at school. I couldn't bear to think that everybody in my class thought as many bad things about me as my family did. Besides, I definitely didn't want any more mistakes going in my Gold Book. 'It takes a billion years for coal to turn into diamonds. I can't wait that long and I want to fast-forward the bad bits,' I complained.

'Can't or won't? Waiting, not knowing, and trusting are all valuable life lessons. They await you, Ruby. When you're ready, they'll appear,' Nettie chuckled.

'Will something bad happen?' I asked. I felt scared again because this didn't feel like something I could plan or have any control over.

'What is the worst thing that could happen to you?' Nettie replied.

'I will get it all wrong, nobody will like me, and I will be sent to my room forever!' As the words left my mouth, I felt shocked. Surely I couldn't think that would be the worst thing, but it is. It is to me because the wretched loneliness broke me over and over. It wore away the good parts of my soul, leaving behind a black nothingness.

'That's nothing you can't handle' Nettie encouraged. 'You've done that loads of times and you're still here to tell the tale.'

'It feels so rubbish. I have no idea what it's all teaching me. It's not like I get angry on purpose, but my family seems to have given me the job of being the angry one.' I moaned.

'The same lesson keeps coming around in a different way until you get the gift. So don't worry, there will be lots of chances. What would it feel like if you expected the best instead of fearing the worst? Have you noticed how you are focusing on the Gold Books and not the rainbow ones?' Nettie observed.

Preparing for the worst was a habit I had learnt from an early age. I was always on guard, alert and ready to face whatever came my way. Like a little soldier going off to war, I put my shield up to protect myself from harsh criticism and fired rounds of angry bullets to keep the enemy at bay.

'My only wish is that they would let me out of that room so I can be with Tom and read my books.' I wished.

'Oh, I think we can do much better than that. The world is your oyster. You can wish for whatever you want.'

I don't believe her. I bite my lip, irritated that I couldn't think of the answer.

'Sit with it, Rubes. It will come. You can't learn if you don't get it wrong. It hurts you because of all the things that happen when you make a mistake. You're only human and I'm afraid that does mean making mistakes. The Gold Books aren't to be used to make you feel bad or to get you to 'do as you're told'. See them more like evidence of how you try to be a good person and all the wonderful things you're learning about life. And pay more attention to the rainbow ones, they are blank pages waiting for your dreams. What do you want for your life?'

I chewed my lip harder. This was going to be a tough two weeks, but with Nettie on my side, I could do it. I had two weeks to get lessons in my Gold Book, or maybe I was going to do Swapsies. *Do you do a Swapsie, or are you a Swapsie? I need to find out more about that.*

'When you've given it some thought, we'll grab a cuppa with The Soul Scroll and see what's occurring. Listen, we need to go back upstairs and get you home,' she raised her eyes to the ceiling.

We left the books to their filing duties. The violet glow of the Life Library began to fade away as I followed Nettie back up the stairs to The Nook.

CHAPTER 7

SHADOW MAN

"Fear is simply excitement without the breath" Fritz Perls

I wasn't expecting to see him when I got back. Getting home from The Wild Wilderness and safely back in my room had been much easier than the tree tunnel drama that took me there. I wrongly assumed that my recent life lessons would prepare me for any darkness, but as usual I was wrong.

In a flash, heart energy had magically transported me to my bed where Tom was sat on my pillow waiting for me. I tickled him under his chin. He stretched his neck out to show his appreciation. I looked at the numbers on the clock. Phew! I was just in time for school. Miraculously, I wasn't feeling tired. In fact, The Wilderness seemed to energise me. Sleep wasn't something I really needed, or so I thought, until I found myself lying in the school medical room under an itchy grey blanket.

I remembered watching Mrs Barnes' cookery demonstration. She had all the ingredients laid out in front of her. Her flowery apron protected her dress and the sleeves of her cardigan were rolled up ready for action. The last thing I heard her say was: 'Today we're going to be making rock buns ...' and then I woke up here. I was crushed because I really enjoyed baking, and I hadn't made rock buns before. Gloria showed us how to bake when we went to stay with her and Sam during the holidays. Baking and sea air held fond memories, but right now, my brain was too foggy to think. I started to feel a bit sick.

The lady from the office behind reception came in and smiled. The overpowering smell of antiseptic and mothballs made it hard to smile back. I dreaded to think when they last washed this blanket—my Mum would not be impressed. She handed me a glass of water and told me I was dehydrated. I remembered having the glass of water at The Nook, but I also felt guilty as I'd had no sleep and no breakfast. I gratefully sipped the water.

'You had a little bump to your head,' she put her hand up to her own forehead to show me where I had fallen. I copied her and felt a gauze bandage covering the left side of my head. 'It was bleeding a bit, but you're okay now. I've filled out a form and we've called your mum. Your dad is coming to collect you. You'll need to drink lots more water and get plenty of rest.' She was stiff and matter of fact. I wondered if poorly children stopped her from getting her chores done. My Dad came and collected me from school. He smiled and ruffled my hair. 'You'll be alright, Rubes!' Then he started the car and turned up the radio. We drove home listening to the football. He must have left the shop early to catch the game. He drove with one hand on the steering wheel, his elbow propped up against the window. It was an automatic drive, so his free hand would intermittently pat my leg and he would smile. My parents were good chauffeurs, they would often taxi me and my sisters about from one club to another. For once, I was glad that my Dad was a man of few words. My head was woozy, and I couldn't concentrate for very long. It was most unlike me. I couldn't remember the last time I didn't feel like talking. Soon we were home and I went to my room and lay on the bed.

The soft pillow held my sore head and I closed my eyes.

I woke up to find a jug of water and orange beaker on the bedside table. My Mum is a nurse and she is good at taking care of me when I am sick. I rubbed my head to find a large bump peeking out from under the gauze bandage. It felt tender and bruised. I slowly sat up in bed and sipped the water. Carefully, I got up to draw the curtains as it was growing dark outside and I felt ready for bed. I changed into my pyjamas and mustered up the energy to go to the bathroom. I didn't want to clean my teeth, but I had drunk a lot of water.

The bathroom was off a small landing halfway between the top and bottom of the stairs. This is where I would often see *him*. I pee a lot before bedtime—it was part of my funny little routine, you know, snow angels to check the duvet, clean feet, and lots of pees. We called them anxi-pees because often there was only a trickle and sometimes nothing at all. I was so worried at nighttime—my body tricked itself into thinking it wanted to go when it didn't. Some nights I would do four or five anxi-pees before I could rest enough to sleep.

Shadow Man was as you'd expect. He was a tall, ghostly, black figure of a man in a long cape and top hat. He suddenly appeared. I couldn't make out his face or any real detail because he was only visible when I looked out of the corner of my eye. Downstairs in the hallway I would glance up at the staircase. As I walked through the hallway to the kitchen, he would appear. In my periphery vision I could make out his floating cloak. My heart would beat fast inside my chest. Like in the tunnel, terror would flood my body and I'd want to run. I wasn't really a screamer when things got scary. The sound would freeze in my throat and nothing came out.

The ever-present but elusive Shadow Man would float along the stairs from the bathroom to the upstairs landing. The faster I ran through the hallway to the kitchen, the quicker he would float. I tried to see through the banisters to get a proper look. The harder I focused, the quicker he would vanish. It was like a game I played. If I ran fast enough would I be free of him?

I couldn't be sure, but I assumed he didn't have legs because his cloak touched the floor and covered where his feet would be. I made up a story in my head that he lived in the toilet because I thought about where he could be when I was in the bathroom and he was nowhere to be seen. My deep-thinking, non-stop brain hadn't yet worked out how the floating cloak got from the toilet onto the staircase. I used the alarm Shadow Man triggered inside of me to do the quickest wees, face washes and teeth cleaning possible. I wanted to stop the nerves pumping around my body and feel safe again.

People in The Hologram House would tease me and say I had a 'vivid' imagination. I thought the joke was on them really because they lived in a permanent land of make-believe. They could cleverly convince themselves, and anybody who would listen, that the Emperor was wearing clothes. That level of denial was off the charts and it was very confusing. Some days, I didn't know which way was up. Even worse, other people, the Hologram Worshippers, actually believed them. Meanwhile, I was seeing real scary stuff that made it hard to sleep at night, and nobody believed me. 'There's a man,' I'd tell my Mum. 'He is going to take me away and I'm scared something bad will happen.' She listened and tried to reassure me. Sometimes I talked to her for hours about the worries in my head, but I wasn't really sure she believed me.

Shadow Man could be felt but not seen in other rooms of the house. I felt his watchful gaze in the lounge when I practised the piano. His overbearing, unwelcomed presence reminded me not to get it wrong. I felt him around me when I was doing dance routines in my bedroom. He felt eerie and scary, as if I could be told off any minute for making a mistake. His piercing stare made sure I was doing it right. Always on show, he never took his eyes off me. He could see me everywhere—he could see if I was being good or bad. I tried to outsmart his fun-sucking, chilling energy by working harder and harder. I thought if I was the best musician, the best writer, the best baker, and the best child, he would leave me alone. I was tired of trying, but not one to give up easily. I was determined to find a way to be perfect. I'd make them so proud of me.

'Are you okay, love?' my Mum called up the stairs from the hallway. I could hear the post-match chat on the TV coming from the lounge behind her. 'Yessss!! I'm going back to sleep.' I put on my best feeling better voice.

'I'll check on you later then,' my Mum joined in the pretence with her nice nurse's voice. She could be really caring at times. 'Night!' I said. I turned out the bathroom light and hurried back to my room, not wanting to make a fuss. I lay in my bed feeling woozy. It took ages to get comfortable and I eventually settled on my side, facing the white fitted wardrobes. It prompted me to think about what I could wear the next time I visited The Wilderness. In my sleep state, I drifted off into a fashion world where I happily styled out my outfits. When I woke up, the evil shadow of the darkness had me in his sights.

Lying on my back, my eyes were barely opened, but I was wide awake. I could feel the blood pumping through my body. There he was. There was Shadow Man standing over me in all his evil finery. I pulled my hands over my face and lay deathly still. I was good at sleeping lions and I had learnt from my dad when watching films, that if it got too scary, you could have a 'cushions up' moment. I wonder what he would call this one, when sheer evil hovered above your bed. I wanted to cry, but nothing came out. My shoulders were all scrunched up and touched my ears. I waited for something bad to happen and release me from the grip of fear. After what felt like hours, but it was probably seconds, I let out a huge sigh. 'My breathing!' I remembered. I tried to inhale and then release. It looked like I was blowing my nose into the palms of my hands. Luckily it was only air and there wasn't any snot or bogies. I thought this was funny and in my relaxed state, the voice inside my head said, *Heart Energy*! I saved myself once again.

Time stood still and I still wasn't feeling brave enough to look. I moved my hands from over my face and placed them across my heart. With my eyes tight shut I inhaled more deeply this time. My jaw clenched, my toes curled over, I prayed with all my might that the heart energy would save me again. *Please*! I pleaded, hoping my whispers would be heard like before in the tunnel.

I opened my eyes and the wicked faceless shadow was still lurking there. I shut my eyes again, unable to move. *What does he want from me*? I wondered. I had a nasty habit of making things my fault and I scrambled around in my memory bank to work out what I could have possibly done this time that deserved this kind of punishment. I was starting to panic again, and my breathing grew short and raspy. I felt like my days were over. Nobody was coming to save me. *Whatever it is*, I bargained with the darkness, *I promise I'll never ever do this again. Just please make this monster go away*!

The light in the hallway came on. My Mum appeared at the doorway with my inhaler in her hand.

'Are you having a bad dream?' she asked as she switched on the bedroom light and came to my bedside. I was genuinely pleased to see her. 'You're very wheezy, Ruby,' she handed me the inhaler and I obediently took two puffs. She pulled the duvet up around me. 'I'll leave the hall light on, darling,' she said, and she went back to bed.

I could no longer see Shadow Man and I wondered if the light really had driven out the evil darkness. Although I was fully awake now and the inhaler had worked its magic. My rattling chest was soothed but I still wasn't alone. I sensed something else in the room.

'Are you okay?' I heard Nettie's voice. I was so relieved. 'I tried to get here as soon as I could. I've been granting wishes.'

'I couldn't reach the moonflower,' I explained. 'My heart energy isn't strong enough to fight off the Shadow Man.'

'Oh, that's Hat Man,' said Nettie as if she was talking about an old friend. 'He often shows up in families as a manifestation of all their fear. It's not your fear, Ruby. When parents haven't faced their fears, their children have to sit in the energy of it with them. Don't worry, your heart energy is working the way it should be. This is something your parents have to deal with. They're so afraid that the lies and secrets of The Hologram House will be revealed and blow their cover, they live in terror. Well, you all do, it's like you're all sitting in a big puddle of fear. It's not much fun living in this perfect world where you don't have permission to freely learn and make mistakes.' She looked sad.

I sat up in my bed and watched her perch on the end of the windowsill. 'When it's your fear, heart energy works a treat. When it's someone else's fear, it's their responsibility to face and overcome it. Everybody has the keys to set themselves free from their own struggles. Nobody can take it away from them—it's one of their life lessons.'

Gold Book, I nodded, understanding what she meant, and also feeling slightly relieved that I could give that job back to its rightful owner.

'If they choose not to face their fear, then all you can do is protect yourself from its dark energy.'

'Why don't my parents face their fear?' I asked.

'Well, that's the million-dollar question, my angel,' she grinned raising one eyebrow. 'It was hard for you to face your fear of the dark when you came through the tunnel to The Wilderness. You had no choice but to face it on your own as part of the test. It made you so angry with me, because you were terrified. Some people have been through a lot of pain and hardship in their life. They think the fear will destroy them, so instead of facing it and understanding it, they've found other ways to block it out.'

'What about their children?' I probed, wondering how adults could have children and not realise how much responsibility and power they had been given.

'Well, you know exactly what that looks like—they are living in darkness too.' She changed the subject, 'Come now. You've really been through the wars today, haven't you?' she was referring to the bump on my head.

'Yeah. I fainted in class today,' I mumbled, embarrassed that she would think I'm a loser. I desperately don't want to disappoint the one adult who has faith and believes in me. 'I missed out on the rock buns.' I complained, swiftly taking the focus off me.

'That's my fault; I didn't get you home in time, did I? All that talk about sugary snacks and then I let you go without rest. I'm sorry. We were having so much fun, I lost track of time. I don't get it right all the time, even though I try. I wanted to show you how to protect yourself, but for now, no more nighttime adventures for you.' she wagged her finger with a cheeky grin pretending to tell me off.

It felt strange to have an adult apologise to me and admit to not getting it right. In my house, adults make all the rules and even when they get them wrong or break them, nobody says anything. There's one rule for them and one rule for us, which presses my 'not fair' buttons. I trust Nettie because the same rules apply to her and she doesn't get angry or make me feel bad for fainting.

'How you feeling now?' she whispered as she sat on the bed with me. She reached up to her crown and pulled out a sprig of purple buds. 'The calming oils of lavender will relax you and help you sleep,' she told me, squeezing the buds between her fingers and wiping them on the edge of my pillowcase. I inhaled the sweetness of the lavender and rested my head back on my pillow.

'Mind your eyes with the lavender!' she instructed snuggling me under the duvet. 'If you're around again soon, we can learn the protection thingamabob.'

'Yes, let's do that. It's the weekend tomorrow!' I couldn't stand the thought of spending another night with Shadow Man. Although now I know what he is, I don't feel as scared. In fact, I'm delighted he isn't my problem and I can tick him off my to-do list.

'How about tomorrow? I could meet you by the fir trees at the end of the garden. Does that work for you?' she hovered over the bed to plant a gentle kiss on my forehead.

'Four pm tomorrow.' I confirmed. My eyes were getting heavy now.

'It's a date,' Nettie said, hopping back onto the windowsill. She activated her heart energy. The room turned violet for a second, and then she disappeared. My eyes were flickering, the lavender felt soothing, and as I sunk deeper into my mattress, I finally fell asleep.

CHAPTER 8

NETTIE'S DAY OUT

The following day at four pm on the dot, I was at the end of the garden ready and waiting. I impatiently wore away the patio stones as I paced up and down along the fir trees. I saw a shiny penny on the floor and picked it up. *Find a penny pick it up, all day long it will bring good luck! I sang to myself.* To kill time, I went over to the shed window and took a sneaky peek at Snowy. Somebody, most likely my Mum had topped up his water bottle with fresh water and filled his cage with more hay. I wondered if Snowy ever got lonely here amongst the cobwebs. I was no stranger to loneliness. Often, I could be in a room full of people and not feel connected to any of them. The fear of them not liking me or making me wrong made me keep my distance. Snowy was like Tom, he didn't judge. I didn't have to mask up around them.

Heart energy! I thought triumphantly. As my thoughts floated off into planning how I could face another one of my fears, Nettie appeared. Pink in the cheeks and breathless, it didn't look like she was going to hang around for long.

'Rubes! There's been a surge of Rainbow Books and we're oversubscribed with wishes!' she panted. 'It was a super New Moon and we've gone into meltdown. We need to call in back-up. I had planned to teach you how to protect your energy today, but sometimes life doesn't work out the way we want it to. That's a whole life lesson in itself!' she laughed at the irony.

'Gold Book,' I nodded.

'Yes, yes, I'm sorry we can't do it today, but I need your help. Are you in?' She shoved what looked like The Soul Scroll into my hands. Cautiously I took it from her, unsure if it was going burst into life. Nettie's head wobbled from side to side as she chattered on, 'I need you to come with me. We're going to round up as much help as possible. I thought we'd start at the Selenite Caves and see how many Mermangels we can find. We can catch a boat from Swift's Bay. We can dunk you in the ocean and give your energy a good clean while we're at it. It has to be clean before we can protect you,' she finished.

I had no idea what she was talking about or what she wanted me to do. I looked down at the sketchy drawing and realised it was a map. I squinted to try and make out some of the places Nettie listed.

Suddenly, my brain was full of questions and thinking of all the things I don't have. I'm not prepared! No swimming costume, no goggles and no towel. I frowned. The face was working overtime.

'... no time to work it out, Rubes. We'll make do with the map, but we have to get cracking. We don't always know how the story ends but we need to give it a go and hope it all turns out the way it's meant to. It usually does,' she spoke quickly. 'Come closer,' she leaned forward to grab my hand. I gripped it tightly, my other hand clutched the map. I was still trying to take in all my instructions and was worried I hadn't understood them properly. 'No time for that, Rubes!' Nettie plucked a moonflower from her crown. She waved it around her head three times as she mumbled some strange language which made no sense to me. The violet glow swirled around us as no sooner had Nettie finished babbling, the ground trembled and we were instantly transported by moonflower power.

There we stood on the sunny shores of Swift's Bay. Palm trees formed a runway down the beach and hummingbird chorus was in surround sound. I could see a hummingbird hovering above the bushes, sipping nectar with its long pointy beak. I remembered reading somewhere that hummingbirds fly backwards. Being so grown up and responsible at a young age was pretty much flying through life backwards. *I must have done lots of the hard stuff already. I've got to the more fun parts now*, I thought.

I bent down to brush off the grains of sand covering my pristine plimsolls. I couldn't bear the thought of them not being white anymore, or even worse, getting gritty sand between my toes. Every year, when we holidayed as a family abroad, I would spend hours on the beach working out how to stop sand finding its way into my beach bag, the pages of my book, and even my bed. This is where my creative problem solving came in. The irritating feeling of sand clinging to my wet feet after a swim, motivated me to come up with a plan. I wanted to be able to cool off in the sea and return to my towel refreshed and sand- less. Quite an impossible task, when there's nothing but a gazillion grains of sand for miles around. No, not for me! It gave me a real sense of purpose to be able to solve this holiday hiccup.

I recalled the time I collected a bucket of sea water to take back to my towel. I would wash my feet once I was settled on the towel with my book. I spread the towel out, brushing off any naughty sand that had snuck in whilst I wasn't looking. I was careful not to shake sand on other people's towels.

With the bucket of water next to me, I slowly lifted up both my feet and balanced on my bottom. Then I lifted the bucket and poured the water on my feet, which were dangling over the edge of the towel. I would shuffle back on my bottom and then place my clean feet down on the towel. Sunglasses on, I could then dry off enjoying my book. Mission accomplished.

It wasn't meant to be a mission, though, it was a holiday. Hardly relaxing or much fun was it, when I was wearing myself out with all these extra jobs to do? No wonder my family hated me so much. I tricked myself into believing that missions made me feel better, when really and truly I was constantly in a state of doing and checking. The checking was bad. Not just once or twice but many times, to be absolutely sure. I couldn't afford to forget because that story didn't end well. I went through a spell of forgetting to take my recorder to school. I never forgot my cello, which was hardly surprising as it was nearly as big as me! It was awkward and heavy which made it a hassle getting it to and from school for my weekly lesson.

Unknowingly, I had turned lots of my life into a mission. Getting ready for bed, making sure my mum was okay, packing my bag for school, and doing my homework, took up most of my time. Doing my hair, riding my bike, and getting dressed, were a close second. The mental checklists in my head could have filled up rolls and rolls of toilet paper. There were too many of them for my young brain to remember. At some point like a laptop with too many tabs open, I was destined to slow down and eventually crash.

As a rule, missions of the Ruby variety generally involved well-thought out, and very detailed plans, which were made well in advance. They were then followed by precision execution and perfect delivery. I could have been a swat soldier. I groaned inwardly at how painstaking and time consuming it was. I hadn't planned for this kind of day out with

Nettie. My clothes were all wrong, I hadn't brought anything with me. If we were going to see people, shouldn't I have my best outfit on and take a gift or some flowers? All this sand was making me itchy.

I turned my attention to the view of the bay. It was a pleasant distraction from all the noise in my head. Just like The Wilderness, the landscape was stunning. It was a sensory delight, as if somebody had turned up all the settings on the television. The colours were brighter, the sun warmer, and the birdsong sweeter. I found the gentle shush of the ocean calming. I noticed a white boat with a striped canopy moored on the rocks nearby. I looked out to sea and watched the waves rise and fall. Up and down they went, never missing a beat. Their consistent turquoise rhythm quelled my anxiety and, without thinking, I placed my hand on my heart. I took in the salty air. It reminded me of the many times we'd been to see Sam and Gloria in their home by the sea. There, I had eaten vinegary fish and chips out of the paper, followed by whippy ice creams with chocolate flakes, and long walks along the pier to play in the arcades.

'Where's the skipper, JB?' called Nettie hurriedly to the pointy-eared fisher boy that I recognised from before. *He must be a Swapsie*, I thought.

'I'm going to take you.' JB clambered into the boat and started the engine.

'Why are you called JB?' I asked as I jumped on board with Nettie. 'I'm Ruby, by the way,' I tell him with my best Show Ruby smile.

'Hi, Ruby! How lovely to meet you. It's a long story but basically when I first arrived at The Wilderness I was like a jumping bean, I was so hopping mad that I couldn't stand still.'

'JB. Ah yes, makes sense,' I replied, wondering what they called me when I first arrived. *If I became a Swapsie, would my ears go all pointy like that?*

'Put your life jacket on. I want to keep you safe and protected. We'll learn more about that later!' Nettie winked. Suddenly the boat moved, we all jolted forward and our speedy flight across the water began.

'Why can't we use heart energy?' I shouted over the whir of the speedboat. Forever curious, I wondered why we had to venture into choppy seas to find the Mer...thing-a-me-bobs. I didn't even know who they were. The not knowing was eating away at me. I was thankful to be away from the sand and checked my plimsolls again. Phew, they were clean.

'You'll see,' Nettie shouted back. She gave me a thumbs up to reassure me.

I started to feel uneasy again, the misty clouds of doubt swirling inside my tummy. Going somewhere new or trying something I've never done before usually makes me nervous. My hands get clammy and my heart beats fast. Going over the plan in my head seems to keep a lid on my worries. I go over and over it until I'm sure, checking that I know what I've got to do. I make sure it's a mission, with lots of time to prepare in advance—what I will wear, what I will take and how much time I'll need. I use my fingers to count the hours and minutes in advance so I'm not late. I hate being late. Suddenly, I realised I didn't have the map. What had I done with it?

We cut through the foamy topped waves—the wind blowing through my hair, the edges of the canopy flapping about overhead. *It does actually feel freeing without a plan*, trying to convince myself I'll be okay without the map. *It's scary and exciting at the same time!*

Nettie's crown held firm her, curls fluttered out behind her. She closed her eyes and looked to the sunny skies. I wondered how I was going to tell her that I'd lost the map. It's not like me to lose things. I couldn't afford to make mistakes and that's why I was usually super prepared. My cheeks flushed with shame. I couldn't believe how stupid I had been. *I've got it wrong again*! I sighed.

We arrived at the entrance to a cave filled with water. JB slowed the boat down and the waves lapped against it. As we bobbed about, JB informed Nettie, 'This is it. I can't go any further.'

'Thank you,' she smiled and said to me, 'Now, Ruby, you're going to put those swimming lessons to the test.'

I gulped.

'Hold on a moment,' she instructed JB. She cupped her hand over her mouth and whistled. I sat there with the tops of my legs trembling. I had been learning to life save and found it really tiring to swim around and around the Olympic-sized swimming pool weighed down by my wet pyjamas. This was to prepare me if I ever had to save somebody and swim with my clothes on. I had wondered when this newly acquired skill would come in handy. I think I was about to find out.

'The saltwater will clean your energy and ground you. Grounding is when you bring your energy back into your body. When your energy is nervous and worried, it's all up here,' she waved her hands frantically overhead as if she was drowning and signally for help. 'It's like you've left your body and we need to bring you back down into your body where you belong,' she pointed to the middle of my chest.

'Okay,' is all I could muster as I was distraught about not having my lucky swimming costume or goggles. The elastic was tightened with precision to fit on my ginger head. I felt totally unprepared without my things. It was uncomfortable being out of my depth. *You don't know ... YOU DON'T KNOW WHAT YOU'RE DOING!!!* my worries screamed.

Nettie whistled again, and then she cupped her hands over her nose and mouth to make strange, high-pitched sounds. It sounded like a squeaky dog toy. I was desperate to work out how she did it. I couldn't work out if the sound was coming from her nose, her mouth, or both. Giving my brain a job to do was a welcome distraction from all the nervy quivers in my tummy. I wanted to do something, anything to make me feel like I was prepared. Doing and thinking about things meant not feeling, and It helped lessen the uncontrollable terror of not knowing.

'Our friends will be along soon,' Nettie announced. I'm none the wiser. The sound of rowdy children echoed in the distance. It was like playtime—squeals, squawks and laughter grew closer. JB drummed his fingers on the steering wheel impatiently waiting to be dismissed. Our friends had finally arrived. Two white bubble-headed creatures poked their heads out of the water and said hello. Nettie greeted the two beautiful icy white Beluga whales as she echoed their clicking and whistling.

'They are called the canaries of the sea because of all the noise they make!' laughed JB.

'They're really big canaries,' I nervously tittered, observing their big wide foreheads and small beak-like mouths. I don't know much about whales, but my noisy brain had already kicked in and it wanted to know if they have teeth. I want it to shut up—I can't have a conversation *and* answer all my brain's questions. 'They look like dolphins with square heads.' I focused my attention back to JB.

'They're very sociable creatures,' Nettie reassuringly chipped in. 'They like to hang out with hundreds of their friends in pods. These two lovelies are our water taxis and they will take us to the Mermangels. She patted their slippery heads, one with each hand.

'Beluga whales stand for the freedom of creativity. You know—letting your mind freely wander into the unknown where magic is made. That's the place in your mind that isn't uptight and worried, Ruby. It's a relaxed state of being, when ideas and projects come to you without much effort at all.'

'Wow!' I leaned forward pretending to be interested, when all I could think about was answering my brain's pesky questions. As I tried to take a closer look, the two square heads disappeared back under the water.

'Whales communicate from the heart and they represent your inner truth. They are all about listening to your feelings and knowing what is right for you. Your creativity and your inner truth will not be silenced. Life has tried to silence you but you're having none of it. Your anger has protected you and kept your truth alive. That's why it's hard for you to let go of it. You have something worth saying and you want people to hear you. Their energy is powerful and strong, can you feel it, Ruby?' Nettie closed her eyes. She had gone off into teaching mode again.

I couldn't feel much, except the impending doom of getting told off. 'I've lost the map,' I blurted, panicking that it's all going to be my fault. I was worried I wasn't going to be allowed to visit the Selenite Caves and wash my energy. I wasn't entirely convinced it needed washing because The Hologram House was a total germ-free zone —the possibility of my energy being dirty was slim. Okay, so occasionally I would wet the flannel and my toothbrush, to make it look like I had washed my face and cleaned my teeth – but let's keep that between us!

JB coughed loudly to get Nettie's attention. She hadn't heard my map confession because she was too preoccupied. I watched her jump onto the head of the first whale and slide down its blubbery body. She made herself comfortable and then turned to me. 'Now you go, Ruby!' She pointed to the second whale. 'You can take Shoukey. He's a bit slower than Orchid.'

I steadied myself on the side of the boat. JB held my arm and Shoukey reversed his body as close to the boat as he could. I gasped dramatically, sucking in salty air through my teeth, my jaw was clenched and my whole body tense. Nettie watched but she didn't say a word. She was willing me on with her smile and kind eyes. I bent down and leant forward. Shoukey lowered his tail fin into the water so I could reach him. I slowly placed my tummy onto Shoukey's bottom and holding on tight with both my hands, I pulled myself along his body until I reached the hole in his head. His wet slippery back was like a slide, but I held firm and pushed up on my hands. As I raised my head, my weight transferred from my tummy to my bottom. Triumphantly, I was slumped over Shoukey's neck hanging on for dear life.

CHAPTER 9

THE SELENITE CAVES

'Ruby!' Nettie yelled. Her cry brought me back into my body. I exhaled sharply. All this time, my focus had been on the task at hand, and in my concentration, I had forgotten to breathe. I let go and my chest deflated. My feet felt freezing cold and I looked down to see my plimsolls having their own swimming pool party in the water below me. There was no time to lose.

'Follow us!' Nettie waved her hand and signalled to the cave.

Shoukey effortlessly pulled away from the boat and I turned around to thank JB. Not wanting to appear rude, I mouthed, 'Thank you!', but JB was already turning the boat around and heading back to Swift's Bay. Shoukey followed Nettie and Orchid who had glided into the mouth of the cave ahead of us.

Moving slowly through the water, I was suddenly overcome by immense gratitude for all the privileges my parents had given me, especially the horse riding and swimming lessons. It turned out that learning to life-save in your pyjamas did have a use after all. I used my riding skills to balance myself on Shoukey. I tightened my tummy muscles, adjusted my seat and gripped Shoukey with my knees. My leggings were soggy against his rubbery skin. As we moved through the darkness of the echoey chamber, the moonflowers in Nettie's crown lit the way. Nettie was right, Orchid was definitely much quicker and he and Nettie took the lead, Shoukey clicked and whistled to his friend as if to say, 'Wait for us!'

Meandering around the wide rocky tunnel, we were greeted by the gentle buzz of the Selenite crystals. Giant criss-cross beams suspended above the water in the ceiling. Sturdy and strong, their milky, translucent structures secured the cave roof over the water. Underneath them was a flat rocky shelf where a Mermangel production was being staged. There were about twenty of them flicking their glossy manes and fluttering their long eyelashes. A cross between an angel and a mermaid, they were stunning!

'So beautiful and elegant!' I remarked as I instantly regretted my outfit choice. I felt dowdy as I admired their twinkly silver robes and long shiny hair tumbling over their fishy tails. My Mum was right—you should wear your best when meeting people you don't know.

I wasn't making a very good impression. *What was I thinking in my damp plimsolls and soggy leggings*? I berated myself. My leggings were starting to dry now and had bagged around the knees. *Why wasn't I more prepared*? I mentally scolded. *I should have been more prepared.*

'Selenite reflected the light. It comes from the Greek Goddess of the Moon, Selene,' said Nettie as she slipped off Orchid's back and landed gracefully on the Mermangel platform. Unruffled by our aquatic adventure, she patted Orchid's head. Then she patted her flowery crown with the other hand, checking that it was still there. Of course it was! This wasn't the first time she had been whale riding.

Shoukey floated patiently by the platform whilst I clumsily tumbled onto the stage, dripping water everywhere. My hair ressembled a dishevelled dog that had travelled at high speed down the motorway with its head hanging out the window. I felt ridiculously out of place and was starting to get a chill. One of the Mermangels handed me a fluffy robe. I removed my life jacket and wrapped it around my goosebumpy skin. Soft and smooth like Tom's furry coat, I was pleasantly surprised to snuggle in and smell vanilla essence, instead of cat breath.

'Hi! I'm Ostara! They call me Starry. Here, give me those,' a raven-haired Mermangel pointed at my feet. 'Let's get you dry. Are you hungry?' she asked, offering me a plate of fresh mango pieces. I stubbornly rejected this service with an illuminating smile. I wasn't ready to let her in. I was more committed to making myself wrong. Even in my family's absence, I was faithful to the rules of The Hologram House. I inwardly cringed at my poor outfit choice and bad manners. I hadn't brought anything with me. I couldn't even remember the stupid map. The voice in my head grew louder, reminding me of all the things I was getting wrong. Like a strict parent it wasn't interested in helping or understanding, it only wanted me to follow orders and do as I was told. I felt helpless to its non-stop nagging.

I obediently handed my shoes to Starry and decided that I did need some refreshment after all. I sunk my teeth into the sweet juicy mango. I was so hungry after the whaling malarkey and I eagerly refuelled my weary body. *You can't even call it a mission because you haven't done your prep and you have absolutely no idea what you're doing*! mocked my inner voice. All this noise in my head made enjoying something new and different really tricky. I tried to distract myself by focusing on what was going on around me.

I thanked Starry who had hung my yellow tinged Plimsolls out to dry. 'Are you a Swapsie?' I asked cautiously. I might have got that totally wrong, but I was curious to learn more.

She shook her head and smiled. I listened intently as she recounted tales about the Mermangels. I was amazed to discover that they are incredibly sensitive creatures with the super-powers of both an angel and a mermaid. Starry proudly told me that it was their job to care for children. She told me how Mermangels are blessed with powerful smiles to instantly reassure children when they're in distress or sick.

Nettie is like that too, I thought. Only she had wings and didn't have a fishy tail. Starry explained to me how she can feel a child's emotions by tuning in to them with her heart energy. She explained that it was a bit like tuning in to a frequency on a radio station with her mind. She was really adamant that the children were not left alone with their struggles and pain. She said that isolation is totally crushing for a human, as they need to be around other humans who can understand and help them.

'What about pets?' I asked, thinking about how Tom was often my saviour in those lonely moments up in my room.

'Yes, pets become like a member of the family and they have their own quirky personalities. Cats and dogs love us without conditions. They don't expect anything more than their food and a cuddle. You know, sometimes we don't need people to do anything but just be there and listen.'

I nodded. Tom was an excellent listener, and he was the only one who could bear to be around me when I was angry or miserable. I loved it when Starry told me that it was her heart's desire to protect children from the darkness whenever she was called. It felt safe knowing that there was somebody kind there for us when we needed them.

'I don't have your number!' I exclaimed!

She giggled. ‘No, Ruby, you call me. You say my name out loud. I’m always listening. I know when you need me and when you can do it for yourself. I believe in you, but if it’s too dark, hand it over to me. Call me!’ she advised.

‘I haven’t thanked Shoukey, I changed the subject and went back to my worried mind which didn’t want me to forget my manners. He looked cute wallowing around in the water with his big melon head and permanently smiling mouth. As he blinked and made more squeaky clicking sounds, I wondered if he was saying ‘Well done, Rubes!’

‘No, well done, you! You were a brilliant water taxi!’ I told him as I patted him gently on the head. He sank back down into the water to join Orchid. ‘Thanks, guys!’ Nettie waved our water taxis goodbye. Their white fins waved back at us as they swam into the vast ocean.

‘How are you feeling, Ruby?’ Nettie asked. ‘All that saltwater is so grounding for your energy. Here, drink this,’ she handed me a glass bottle of distilled water. ‘Do you still feel nervous or worried?’

I realised that my brain hadn’t asked a question for at least two minutes. The bloating-something bad-might-happen feeling had eased in my tummy.

My breathing was calmer. I placed my hand on my heart and zoned into my body. 'I think I'm good!' I said.

'Just good?' Nettie pushed. 'What does good mean?'

'It means I'm safe,' I replied grumpily. I don't like being challenged. It makes me feel like I've got it wrong again. My curiosity kicked in. 'Well, maybe *this* is happy. What do you think?' I asked Nettie, eager to see if she thinks this expansive feeling in my chest could be happiness.

'It could be, sweetie. I can't possibly know how you feel. Only you know what it's like to be in your body. Everybody has their own kind of happy. You weren't very happy when I made you come on this adventure,' she said crinkling up her nose. It was her turn to pull a face! She continued, 'We didn't use heart energy because I wanted you to step out of your comfort zone and face uncertainty without a plan. I wanted you to know that you could do it. I wanted you to feel the pride and joy of beating your fear. I wanted to see you succeed and I thought if you were helping others, you would be more likely to do it.'

'It was another test?' I said, exasperated. I hate not knowing. I wasn't angry, but I felt silly. I backed away from the Mermangels and wished this conversation could be more private. Nettie read my discomfort and lowered her voice. 'It's one for your Gold Book, Ruby! You showed me how big your brave is even when you felt wobbly. You worked it out on the spot without any help. If I had told you that we were coming here, would you have believed me? Would you have wanted to come?'

'What is my comfort zone?' I avoided her question and dismissed all the praise she was giving me.

'Everything we do repeatedly becomes familiar and comfortable—this is your comfort zone,' she explained. 'When we step outside of what we know, when we try something new, meet new people or visit a place we've never been—like swimming with Shoukey and Orchid—this is outside of your comfort zone. You don't get to experience the amazingness of life if you don't dare to step outside of your comfort zone. Even staying curious and asking all the questions like you do, Ruby, is one step closer to moving outside of your comfort zone because you know there is something else out there other than what you know. There's so much we don't know. Nobody can know everything.'

‘I annoy people with my questions,’ I put myself down again. I was clearly not ready to change my mind. I stubbornly stuck to being wrong because ironically, it feels familiar and comfortable!

‘There aren’t many things that are certain in life,’ Nettie looked up to the sky and said, ‘The sun sets and rises, the waves rise and fall,’ she paused. ‘You are born, your heart beats until it’s your time. You don’t know when your time will come,’ she concluded.

‘Cheery!’ I joked sarcastically. I didn’t like to think about death. I think the closest I had come to it was when Shadow Man paid me a visit. ‘Anyway, I made a mistake. I lost the map,’ I confessed still wanting to make myself wrong.

‘Maybe you didn’t need the map,’ she winked.

‘No map. No comfort zone. Only a crazy person would do that!’ I defended my wrongness.

She raised her index finger and eyebrows at the same time. ‘We’re all a little crazy. The crazy ones are the ones who do it differently. They change the world. Those gifts you get for being brave and stepping outside of your comfort zone far outweigh the temporary fear. The lessons you learn are worth it. You are worth it, Ruby.’

'What if you're permanently scared?' I asked tearing up as I realised that I spend most of my time in my comfort zone, small and alone, fearing that I'll get it wrong and people will harshly judge or punish me.

'Feelings are temporary, lovely Girl,' she leaned in and enveloped me in the fluffy robe. She squeezed me tight. 'Those scared feelings are simply energy passing through your body. They can't hurt you. The fear may bubble away under the surface but with courage that is what leads you to joy and love. Love is stronger than fear. The energy of those feelings vibrates at a higher frequency. Those feelings are the powerful bright lights in the darkness.'

'I see,' I swallowed, trying to blink back the tears. I feel relieved to know that I'm allowed to have all these feelings. *Human beings are very complicated!* I thought as I let go of the wrongness.

'Tissue?' she handed me one and asked jokingly, 'The million-dollar question, Ruby—is it one for your Gold Book?'

I couldn't answer the question as tears were streaming down my face, 'It's not funny! I can't believe I went swimming with my clothes on. My plimsolls are ruined! It looks like somebody has peed on them. The saltwater has turned them yellow. What will I tell my Mum? It's so unfair, you didn't give me the chance to make a plan. Not even a little plan. It was such a mission and I made a terrible outfit choice. I didn't wear my best clothes to meet new people, and they all looked so glamorous. I had no gifs to offer when I got here, and I swam with animals I knew nothing about—they could have eaten me!' I gabbled, frustrated and confused.

'And ..?' Nettie raised her eyebrows again, waiting for me to fill in the blanks.

'I'm having such a wonderful time. I could only dream of doing stuff like this. Riding a Beluga Whale in the beautiful ocean, meeting Mermangels and basking in the energy of those massive crystals. It did go wrong, but at the same time, it went *very, very* right,' I finally admitted. No sooner than my frustration had been expressed, it melted away.

'You did. You took to the water with Shoukey like you've been riding whales all your life! It was totally awesome! 'What does that really mean?' Nettie asked. 'Does getting it wrong matter?'

'Not really. When I am prepared, I still get things wrong,' I acknowledged. I recalled the time I had spent ages making the house tidy for my Mum and she still sent me to my room because I answered her back. 'When things don't go the way they are meant to, they are wrong. People only notice the things you do wrong, they don't notice all the things you do right.'

'Do you notice what you do right?' Nettie asked. I shook my head. I looked down at my bare feet. 'I only see the bad stuff, what isn't quite right or what needs changing.' I wrung my hands together under the fluffy blanket.

'Anyway, who gets to decide what is right or wrong?' Nettie asked.

'Urrrm, I dunno,' I mumbled awkwardly. I hate not knowing still. 'It's just the way my parents have raised me to be a good kid.'

'You are a good kid. Even without perfect plimsolls, the plans, the fancy clothes. Even when you forget things or you don't know, you're still a good kid. It's not your job to know it all and you can't know it all. You're still young, there's plenty of time to learn,' she reassured.

'You *really* **ARE** a good kid, Ruby. You're kind, smart, brave, and funny. You have good manners because you naturally care about how other people feel. Today, you tried something new. There was zero planning and we're all good,' she air-quoted my choice of words and giggled.

I giggled too. 'What a waste of your beautiful brain and your precious life worrying about things, just in case,' she concluded. 'Isn't it?!'

I agreed. I was still giggling. 'I can't believe I do that. It's nonsense.'

'It's not nonsense, Ruby. You like to know what's coming next. Not knowing feels scary. It does for lots of us. It's your way of coping when you feel scared,' she explained. 'You don't know what you don't know. We're all writing in our Gold Books. Learning what you don't know can be fun and scary at the same time. Repeat after me, 'It's safe for me to not know, because I'm smart and I can figure anything out.''

I repeated her words aloud. We had taken the scenic route, but finally, I had reached the point where I could feel proud of my efforts. Maybe I wasn't a lost cause and I could get the hang of feeling scared and excited at the same time. It would take some practice, but I was determined.

'Are we doing the protection thing today?' I asked, feeling more confident and ready for more.

'I think that's enough for one day,' she replied. 'I've got a crystal recording you can take home and listen to. It's pretty straight forward. You can learn it for yourself and get some practice in.'

'Wha …' I was about to ask her another question. I thought better of it. 'I'll figure it out,' I grinned. 'I'm a smart kid,' I whispered, playfully mimicking her voice.

The Mermangels huddled around us—the smell of vanilla essence and saltwater was good enough to eat. Starry grabbed my plimsolls, and as I tied my laces, I noticed they were dry. I hoped and prayed they were white enough to pass the Mum test.

'I'm heading back to The Wilderness with these guys,' Nettie announced into the crowd of Mermangels. 'You need to go home and get some rest,' she said to me, handing over a clear crystal. I put it in my pocket and removed the fluffy robe. I gave it back to Starry and thanked her for taking care of me.

'We've got work to do!' The Mermangels clapped their hands with sheer delight, whoops and happy screams echoed around the cave. 'The New Moon energy lasts for three days, so we still have time to file all the Rainbow wishes.'

'Let's go!' And with a blast of heart energy, they were gone.

I stood there realizing that my time was running out too. Tick Tock! *Was I destined to become a Swapsie?* It seemed like a cowardly way to leave without saying a proper goodbye. I'm not very good at leaving or ending things. I wasn't sure I was ready to leave my family, but living with them was tricky. I was miserable shut away in my room, I was very angry with them, as they were with me.

Did I have other choices? Was there another way? What else could I do? I sure had tried my best to get on with them and make them happy. I had failed. It was possibly the worst mistake I had ever made. Perhaps it was one I wouldn't be able to put right.

CHAPTER 10

THE PROTECTIVE POWER SUIT

I opened my eyes and I was sharply returned to the chaos of The Hologram House.

'RUUUUUBBBBEEEEEEEE!' my Mum bellowed up the stairs. Her outdoor voice, which technically she should not be using inside, had the power to break through walls as it boomed down the corridor to my bedroom. I rushed to the top of the stairs to head it off.

'YESSSSSS!' I hollered back.

'I've been calling you for ages. What are you doing up there?' I can see the top of her blonde hair furiously wobbling about while she stood at the bottom of the stairs. She drummed her manicured fingers on the banister. I held my breath.

She didn't wait for my reply but started her usual rant. 'Why don't you come the first time I call you? I'm sick of you. All of you! You just TAKE, TAKE, TAKE,' she emphasised the words moving her head backwards and forwards like a clucking chicken. 'You're so ungrateful. This is not a hotel. I spend my whole life picking up after you. I've never met such a bunch of selfish kids in my whole life.'

I had heard this one before, and I wanted to say: 'Don't be so bloody melodramatic,' like she says to me when I get angry. She had taught me good, but I was smarter than that. I sighed.

'Soooorrrrrry Mum.' I stood there willing her to stop. Sorry was like a white flag in our house and it saved you when your bottom was literally on the line. Sorry could stop that big wooden spoon from coming off the wall and taking you out. Sorry to me wasn't about apologising for something I hadn't done wrong. No, it meant I surrender, leave me alone. I said 'Sorry!' without meaning it on countless occasions.

My mind started to drift as she ranted on. I wondered why she hadn't worked out that I don't listen to her. There's no point—whatever I do, however hard I try, she still seems to find something wrong or incomplete. She's a slave to the neverending to-do list and I'm not signing up for that, but I don't have a choice. I'm tired like she is. The call of The Wilderness was becoming more and more appealing.

'Make yourself useful—put this washing away!' she snapped, shoving a pile of neatly ironed clothes on the bottom of the staircase. She stormed off and I counted to ten, waiting until the coast was clear. I reluctantly collected the washing. It was still warm and smelt of fabric softener. I quickly distributed each item to its rightful room. White work shirts hung on my parents' bedroom door, little bundles of socks and folded parcels on each person's bed, ready for them to tidy away in their rightful homes. Everything has a home. Everything must be put back in its home so it can be found when we need it. I like that. It feels good to know where things are. It also creates drama when things go missing. It's far smarter to find the right home than pay the consequences.

When I had finished my chores, I executed the perfect swan dive onto my bed and realised how grumpy I was to be back home. I thought about how my parents say the same lines over and over. Their trademark catchphrases play on a loop, going around and around, keeping them locked into a cycle of misery and dissatisfaction.

Nothing changes for them or for me. There must be another way, another choice. There is always another way, I pondered. I'm continually searching for different and better ways. I truly believe that things aren't simply done one way and that's the end. I don't accept how things are on the surface—I want to dive deeper and work it all out.

My Mum felt unappreciated, tired and ignored. My Dad demanded respect and obedience. 'Do as you're told! Rules are rules!' he would bark. I wished I could make them see that it wasn't too late to learn. It was like they were frozen in time, too rigid to grow and mature. It was too sad to think that the pages of their Gold Books were left unwritten.

You don't know what you don't know! Nettie had taught me as I scolded myself in the Selenite Caves for getting it wrong. Except I wasn't wrong, I was doing it differently. I was finding my own way. Nettie didn't make different wrong. She made different acceptable. It is courageous to forge your own path and stand out from the crowd.

My parents were keeping themselves trapped by stubbornly refusing to learn. Their rigid approach kept them safe from the uncertainty of change—from doing it differently. It was easier to expect other people to change and do the work. All the time they blamed me and other people, all the time the rest of the world was wrong, they remained stuck. They have a choice. It seemed ridiculous to me that they were giving their power away like that. Why haven't they put those lessons in their Gold Books? What made them let fear close off their hearts?

I rummaged in my pocket for the crystal. I felt positive and confident that I could work out how to learn how to protect my energy by myself. Initially, I was excited about learning something new, but then gave up after my first attempt. I closed my eyes and held the crystal over my heart. I waited. Nothing. I couldn't concentrate. Somebody was coming down the hallway. I impatiently tossed the clear quartz on the pillow behind me.

'Hello, Tom!' I exclaimed, pleased to see his friendly furry face as he curled his body around the door and purred. I patted the bed, coaxing him to join me for a cuddle. Tom is my comfort blanket and I love hanging out with him. His soft chubby body is warm and soothing.

'How was your day?' I whispered as I lie back on my bed. He wrapped himself around my pillow, purring in my ear, his whiskers tickling my face.

'You wouldn't believe where I've been!' I exclaimed. "It's a magical world out there. Not like in here." Tom doesn't know about The Hologram. He doesn't fault-find, criticize, or insist I show up a certain way. He looked deep into my eyes, listening intently. I adore his deep, cat eye stare. His clear yellow eyes gently look at my soul in a reassuring way. He is the only one I can make direct eye contact with for any length of time and not feel bad inside.

I melted into the mattress, wanting to spend time reliving my ocean adventure. I remembered Nettie's glowing praise and how good it had felt to hear I had done something right. *Self-praise is no recommendation*, said the voice in my head. It's another one of my Dad's quirky sayings. I think it means don't be a show-off. I am a show-off though. I love to dance in front of an audience, and I love to tell people about all the things I have learnt. I want them to learn new things too. What's wrong with having a smart voice and wanting to use it for good?

Tom made a funny noise. It was a deep noise that seemed to be coming from his tummy. 'Are you hungry?' We're still locked in our cat stare, but the noise is not rumbletums, it's music. I glanced over at the windowsill half expecting to see Nettie. Then I remembered she had taken the Mermangels back to The Wilderness. My super alert detective skills kicked in and were now on red alert. I glanced back to Tom. The music had stopped, his tummy started to speak.

"Learning to protect your energy is very important for Wildhearts!" said the deep voice.

I pulled a face. The voice continued: ***"Wildhearts are very sensitive to the energy around them. There are a few ways you can protect your energy and today I'm going to show you how!"***

I laughed. Tom was not talking to me! 'Move your big tum!' I told him playfully as I pulled out the crystal from where he was sitting. My breathing kicked in and I was momentarily taken off red alert. I put the crystal close to my ear on the pillow beside me and continued to stroke Tom's tummy. I eagerly tuned in to the crystal recording and discovered how to protect my energy.

I woke up fully clothed on top of the duvet. Daylight peered through a crack in the curtains and

I looked for Tom. I patted the duvet, half asleep searching for his furry warmth. He must have gone for breakfast. It's Sunday. There is no school. I sprang out of bed and noticed the quartz crystal on the floor next to my slippers. I picked it up and shoved it in my drawer. I still hadn't found the courage to tell my family about Nettie and The Wilderness. Every time I went to share, something stopped me. I was scared they wouldn't believe me and would use it as a form of punishment.

The smell of sizzling sausages wafted up the stairs. I changed out of my crumpled clothes into my pyjamas so I could beat the gannets. That's what family mealtimes are like. We swarm to the table and eat as if we'll never eat again. I don't know why because there isn't a famine and we're not on rations. Quite the opposite, the fridge is full of enough food to feed a small country. My Mum's compulsion to shop is as big as her compulsion to clean and tidy. I live in fear of being hoovered up, and often worry she will whip my plate away from under my nose, mid sausage! The sausages are from my Dad's shop and everybody who has ever eaten them says they're the best. I agree. I watched a man make them one day when I was visiting the shop. I didn't see the secret ingredients but the way he made them was mind-blowing. With the agile fingers of an illusionist, he speedily took lumps of pink squidgy pork and magically transformed them into strings of skinny sausages right before my eyes.

Down in the kitchen, my Dad and the girls were seated around the table, tucking in. My Mum was in her usual position at the sink wearing her yellow rubber gloves. She had been on Nurse duty these past few days bringing food to my room and checking on me. Nettie and I had made it look like there was a body under the duvet using stuffed toys and clothes. We found a doll with the same colour hair as me and left the head peeking out the top of the duvet so it looked like I was asleep. I'd seen it in a movie before and thought it was such a clever trick. I felt dishonest, but I wasn't going to miss out on having fun with Nettie.

'How's your head, love?' my Mum turned around from the washing up and smiled.

'I'm all good, thanks Mum,' I said not wanting to get into it. My appetite was back and I was eager to get started. Jemima and Jaz smiled at me as I sat down at the table. I helped myself to thickly buttered granary bread and three sausages. I smothered them in tomato sauce, hoping nobody would notice. *They don't make sausages like this in The Wilderness!*

Unfortunately, it was Jemima's turn today. 'No singing at the table!' my Dad lifted his head from the newspaper long enough to tell her off. Jemima's smile turned into a glare. My dad eats like a hungry horse at a trough, his lips smacking together as he slurps his coffee in between bites. Apparently, he is allowed to make a noise eating in this way, but when I noisily enjoy my cooked breakfast or my sister sings, that's bad manners.

'Would you like some sausages with your sauce?' Jaz mocked sarcastically and loud enough for him to hear. I knew this tactic only too well. She was trying to take the heat off Jemima and get me into trouble.

'Pack it in you two!' barked my Dad with a mouthful of sausage. He turned the page of the Sunday papers. We have three of them delivered on a Sunday so that keeps him very busy. My Dad is allowed to read the paper, but we can't sing. There are restrictions around tomato sauce.

Section 3.2 of the Condiments Act: 'Though shalt not smother one's sausages on a Sunday'.

The whole thing is ridiculous! I thought to myself, angry at the injustice of all these unwritten rules with different variants for each member of the family. *How can we get it right if we don't even know what they are? Maybe my Swapsie was to trade in the world's yummiest sausages for some straight-forward fair rules!* I scoffed my breakfast down as quickly as possible, followed by enough apple juice to ward off indigestion, and asked to leave the table. Permission granted, I stacked my plate and glass neatly in the dishwasher and skipped safely back upstairs.

On the way back upstairs, I popped into the bathroom to clean my teeth and wash my face. I hadn't seen the Shadow Man since that fateful black night, but I was still wary that he might be lurking. I didn't hang about. When I got back to my room, Tom was waiting for me on my pillow. He watched me retrieve my diary from under my mattress. That's its special home that nobody knows about except me. Not much is private in The Hologram House because all plans, thoughts, deeds and words need to be openly shared and given the stamp of approval by the people in charge. They have to meet the required standards of perfection and follow the script. To add another layer of complication and mystery, this script isn't written anywhere, so it's a silly guessing game. It's not a fun game, not one I liked to play.

My head is full of information. I don't know how I hold it all up there. There are rules and funny sayings to remember. There are things I must say and things I cannot say. There are important dates like birthdays, Mother's Day and Father's Day. There are all the good manners I've been taught: 'Please and thank you', 'Please may I leave the table', 'Thank you for having me'. There are all the times I must remember to smile when I don't feel like it, and all the times I must talk to people who visit our house, when I'd rather go and sit with Tom in the playroom and read my books.

There are all the sounds that I need to watch out for—any sound that means my Dad is not asleep or reading the paper. Like his car in the driveway, his loose change rattling in his pocket, the kitchen chair scraping on the tiles as he gets up from the kitchen table. There are all the 'right' ways I must do things. It's lazy if you don't do them thoroughly enough—empty the dishwasher, hang out the washing, clean the toilet, vacuum the lounge, make your bed, do your homework, put away your toys and clean washing properly. There are all the homes of all the items in the house to remember, so you could return them to where they belong.

The tricky bit is anticipating all the tasks I don't know yet. I haven't had any psychic training, but I have learnt how to mind read. I know when my Mum is sad, angry, or she needs me to help her. I have learnt that sighing and banging things about was a sign it was time to step in. I was pretty good at working it out, even when there was no sighing. Silence was worse really, because you knew something bad would follow. I could see when her face or voice changed, and I knew what each subtle expression meant. I would know in a split second if I should stay and fight or run away.

My head could get a bit overloaded, so it's no surprise I find school a struggle. I have a tutor to help me with that and I find writing things down really helps. I took out my diary, so I could write down the crystal recording before I forgot.

'You never forget the things you're meant to remember!' Nettie appeared from behind the curtain and had been standing there for some time watching me furiously filling up the pages of my diary. I was startled and worried we would get caught. I rushed to shut my bedroom door. 'What you need to know, your brain remembers. It won't forget. Really! I promise. Trust me! You don't need to force it and try so hard, Rubes. Trust yourself!' She made a T shape with her two index fingers.

'I have all this stuff in my head,' I started to tell her. I wondered if she would think I was stupid and if everybody has stuff to remember. I don't want to make a fuss and think better of it.

'What stuff?' she pressed. 'Things you've learnt at school? Lessons and facts?'

'Nah,' I hesitated. 'I have a lot to remember to help my Mum, so she doesn't freak out.' I left out the other stuff. There weren't enough hours in the day to tell her all of it.

'Oh, sweetie! I think your Mum is under a lot of stress. When everything has to be so perfect and right, I can only think your Mum creates a lot of unnecessary work for herself. She's doing what she knows. You only know what you know. This is her way and, yes, there are other ways but only she can discover that.'

I sighed. 'I feel bad now. I know my Mum tries hard. I know my Dad works hard. I know she doesn't mean to be a stress-head.' I always defend her in the end. It comes back down to the simple fact that she is my Mum and I'm meant to be on her side. Even when she's not on mine. I understand her and I don't think for one moment she enjoys hurting me.

'You can protect yourself from that.' she reassured me.

I tried to remember what the crystal recording said. My head was like fuzzy cotton wool. I pulled a face. I vaguely recalled that I had to use the power of my imagination and focus my mind on what I wanted to feel—safe, and not what I feared.

'What did you choose to protect yourself—the bubble, the rainbow, the Power Suit or something else?' Nettie enquired.

'I wasn't sure the bubble would work,' I told her. 'To be honest, having everybody see in, felt scary and it didn't feel strong enough. I need something stronger. The rainbow is a nice idea. I love rainbows. Their bright colours make me happy.' I stopped and looked at her to make sure I'm remembering it right.

'I went for the Power Suit,' I concluded. 'Not that I think I'm a super-hero or anything. Far from it, but I reckon that wearing a zip-up babygrow that covers me from head to toe would be the safest thing.'

'Great! Whatever works for you.' Nettie smiled and put her thumbs up.

'I want my Power Suit to be pearly white and shimmering in moonflowers,' I told her. I had already styled it out in my mind.

'That sounds awesome! I love it! Like a spacewoman! You know, once you start remembering to imagine putting that on every day, and you have less of other people's stuff in your energy field, you will feel so much better. You will be able to listen to your own feelings. You may even feel less angry. Your energy field—or aura as we call it—is made up of how we feel in the moment. It's not visible to the naked eye, but it is different colours. Other people's auras can merge with ours and that's why we need to protect ourselves. Wildhearts are very sensitive and they pick up on other people's feelings and energy when they are close by.'

It was all coming back to me now, Nettie was right, you didn't forget what your brain wanted you to remember. 'If I can't see it, how do I know what colour my aura is,' I asked her.

'Tune into your heart energy and ask your body how it feels. The answer will come. If you keep listening to the crystal recording it will tell you what all the different colours mean.'

'I have a feeling my aura is red,' I said thinking about all my angries and how big they could get.

'Mmm, I wonder if it's a mixture of colours,' Nettied wondered

'What, like a rainbow?' I imagined myself sitting in a rainbow coloured light.

'Wildhearts have indigo in their auras. The indigo means you are an independent thinker with great wisdom. You were born knowing stuff that you don't need to learn. You have deep integrity and sincerity. You only do and say things that you mean. You want the world to be fair and you are a defender of people's rights to the end.'

I feel a bit overwhelmed. 'I don't have any Epsom salts to put in my bath,' I panicked remembering when the crystal recording had given care instructions. 'How can I keep my aura free from other peoples' ickiness if I can't clean it properly?'

'In the morning when you take a shower, imagine a bright white or golden light washing away all the negative energy. That's an easy one to do because you have a brilliant imagination. You have a shower every day, don't you?' she looked at me suspiciously and then grinned. She could be quite mischievous at times and it was as if she already had a knowing about my rushed visits to the bathroom.

'Not today!' I held my nose and pretended to waft away an invisible stink with my hand. 'I fell asleep in last night's clothes,' I giggled.

'That reminds me, I have something to give you,' Nettie looked proud as she handed me a rucksack. It was just like hers with the same embroidered 'W' on the front pocket.

'Open it,' she urged as I stood there frozen to the spot.

'Thank you!' I exclaimed, composing myself. I opened the rucksack and laid its contents out on the bed whilst Nettie gave a running commentary.

There was a Selenite wand. It was much smaller than the giant beam-like structures that had held up the caves. 'It's a baby wand for you to carry with you,' she told me excitedly. 'It radiates light against darkness, and it also opens up your intuition. Your intuition is like a Satnav, guiding you and showing you the way. It helps you tune into your feelings, instead of everybody else's.'

'Wow!' I held the crystal up to the window and felt its calming energy.

'All crystals have different energies for different purposes. The clear quartz I gave you empties your mind, and it brings clarity which can be super helpful when you're learning. I thought that might help with your homework.'

I was prone to having huge meltdowns on a Sunday evening before homework was due. My sausages would repeat on me as I made myself sick with worry that I was doing it wrong.

'That one is rose quartz. That is love, Ruby. Love heals all suffering—sadness, loneliness, anger and fear.'

I gently take the pale pink stone from her and wonder at how something so small can be so powerful.

'Small and mighty like you!' Nettie laughed.

'You think?! I doubt it,' I teased, more comfortable putting myself down and deflecting the compliment.

'You're a lot stronger than you know, Ruby. I've already seen your inner strength. It doesn't have to be big and loud. It just needs to show up when it matters most,' she said.

I told her about the kids in my class and how I think Annie, Poppy, and Callum were brave to deal with big life lessons when they are so young. She listened and smiled. She nodded her head and said, 'See! Already you're so wise—this is your inner knowing. Children know things without learning them or being told by grownups. In fact, life is their best teacher. They see things, they feel things, they know. Grownups sometimes interfere too much. They don't mean to, but they do. Sadly, children who suffer big losses early on in life can be pained by them forever if they do not turn them into lessons for the Gold Book.'

Nettie returned to the gift giving. 'Ah, now these are fun, and they helped me a lot. I was a lot like you, Ruby, not sure of myself and looking for answers,' she pointed to a silver matchbox inscribed with the word 'Ask' on the front. I slide the box open and inside were lots of cards with handwritten messages.

'When in doubt—ask and the answer will appear!' Nettie told me. 'Tap the box, take out the cards, ask a question!' she instructed.

'Why do you tap the box?' I asked while I watched her shuffle the cards. 'You have to put your energy into the cards, so the right answer will appear.'

I frown, not sure if I believe her. 'Is it a magic trick?'

'It feels like magic,' she answered. 'What shall we ask? Okay, let's think of a question. What do we need today to help us trust more?'

'Good question!' I said as Nettie closed her eyes and held the cards face down over her heart.

'You know the answers, they are in your heart, Ruby, but sometimes, we block them and we need a little help. There's nothing wrong with asking for help.'

She pulled out a card and read it to me. ***'Life is magical and fun. Believe that anything is possible. Find ways to see the magic and trust it is there!'***

Wide-eyed and full of disbelief, I stared at the card. 'That's incredible. How do they know?'

'Our thoughts are made up of energy too. The cards mirror back to us what we need to know. Life does that too. What we see in others, we have inside of us. You know those kids in your class—you're just as brave as them. You see it in them because you have so much courage in you. It's just you need to believe that to be true.'

'The anger. I see the anger in my Mum. I have that in me too,' I said thinking that perhaps we were more alike than I wanted to admit.

'You do, poppet, and like your Mum, you have valid reasons to be angry. The anger is not wrong—

it's a message for you to change something. It's about learning how to listen to your anger, and how to use the energy in a way that doesn't hurt other people.'

'The fear. I see the fear in my Dad. I have that in me too,' I acknowledged, wondering if my Dad had ever seen a Shadow Man when he was a little boy.

'You certainly do. You've been raised in a house full of fear, so naturally you're scared too. What's amazing is that you're learning how to show up in spite of the fear. It's all turning out the way it's meant to.'

I fan the cards out across my duvet, all their little messages staring back at me and giving me hope. 'Thank you so much, Nettie,' I said. 'Thank you doesn't feel like it's a big enough word. You're so kind to me. I'm really lucky to have met you.'

Her face was beaming. 'There's one more. Where is the lip balm?' She retrieved a small round pot from the bed and handed it to me.

'It will help you remember your kind words, even when you're angry. I know you don't mean it, but words sting and once they're out, you can't put them back in.' I squirmed—I've got it wrong again. 'We all say and do things in the heat of the moment,' Nettie reassured me. 'It's salted caramel—your favourite.' She looked pleased with herself.

I smeared some of the ice cream flavoured 'Caramella' on my lips and smacked them together. 'Lush!' I pouted, kissing the air.

I began to tell Nettie the story of the scrumpled paper that I had learnt at school. She listened intently as I recalled the time Mrs Barnes had given us each a clean sheet of paper from her note pad. She had told us to scrunch it up and jump on it. Then had made us smooth it out on the desk in front of us. She had then explained to us how unkindness is not reversible, even when we say sorry. Just like the creases on a piece of paper can still be seen, even when you smooth it out again.

As we sat on the end of my bed, I talked about all the horrible things I've said to my Mum and all the insincere sorries I had traded for some peace and quiet. I wondered how many horrible words were said to my Mum when she was growing up. I thought about all the times her cruel words had hurt me.

'We've scrunched each other up and now we can't unscrunch!' I declared. 'I'm one of those socks in your boot that's falling down—tolerable but uncomfortable and definitely annoying. When you get the chance, you know that you will whip it off and find a better pair of socks. I get in the way, my feelings are an inconvenience,' I told her.

Nettie was holding up a t-shirt like the one JB was wearing when I first met him. It said *'Strong Belief - Wild Heart'* in gold letters across the middle. I took it from her and ran my finger over the gold lettering.

'That gets me into so much trouble,' I sighed.

'That is your gift.' Nettie stuck up for me. She wouldn't let me put myself down so easily. 'I want to teach you how to channel that wild strong energy for good. It's the energy of a fierce leader who wants to make change in the world,' she said.

I gulped. 'That feels a bit scary for a girl like me.'

CHAPTER 11

THE EXTRAORDINARY EXPERIMENT

Nettie nodded and when I'd finished talking, she leant forward. I talked about my Mum and how she buys such thoughtful gifts. She loves to give gifts. Both my parents are very generous. I've never wanted for anything. I never went without. My eyes filled up with tears. 'My Mum puts gifts like the ones Nettie had given me in our Christmas stockings and she spends ages planning our birthdays.'

'This is the way she shows love,' Nettie remarked.

'And with food,' I broke my sadness with a laugh and patted my tummy. 'I don't think I feel love in that way.' I said.

'You both have different love languages. A bit like a Spanish person talking to a French person—nothing makes sense.'

I burst out laughing. 'That sounds about right. My Mum doesn't really get me, and I can't work her out either.'

'I have an idea!' Nettie declared with a mischievous glint in her eyes. 'How do you fancy being a Scientist?' Nettie's voice speeds up when she is excited. 'Right! I'm going to shrink myself so I can climb inside your ear. I pulled a face. *What was she up to?*

'You won't feel a thing, but you'll be able to hear everything I say. We need a few props for this experiment.' she explained.

She removed her flowery crown and placed it down on the floor in front of her. As she went to jump inside it, I thought *There's no way she is going to fit in there!* I was wrong! *Ouch!* Before my very eyes, Nettie was magically transformed to the size of a thimble. I picked her up and placed her gently in the palm of my hand. Before I could start asking questions, she squeaked 'Put me on your shoulder!' Her high pitched voice reminded me of the time I sucked the helium from one of my birthday balloons. Like the singing chipmunks, my sisters and

I found it too funny. We had a bad case of the giggles that day!

I put Nettie up on my shoulder, but as I turned to see what she was doing, she had vanished!

'Nettie!' I called. I looked over my other shoulder. *Where had she gone?* 'I'm in here!' echoed the mouse like voice from inside my head. I put my finger in my ear and wiggled it around. It felt itchy.

'Hey! Careful! You'll push me too far in and I won't be able to get out.' *Whoops!* My Mum had warned me about doing this with cotton buds when I cleaned my ears out.

'Sorry!' I said, and I really meant it. I didn't want to hurt Nettie.

'Ewwww! When did you last clean your ears?' Nettie complained. 'It's so busy in here, Rubes! Your brain is constantly locked into worry mode. No wonder you're so uptight and angry. I'm going to try and disconnect it for a while so you can follow my instructions.'

Aaaaah that feels better! It was like Nettie had flicked a switch and I felt all calm and relaxed. 'What did you do?' I asked her, wondering if this was something I could for myself.

'It's magic. Focus on taking deep breaths. Now, can you fetch three coins and three containers!'

instructed Nettie. *What is she up to?* I thought suspiciously. I skipped down the stairs, passed the bathroom into the lounge. I wasn't scared of Shadow Man and even had a little smirk on my face. It was my secret. I don't think anybody would believe me if I told them that I had a teeny tiny fairy inside my head. I quickly rummaged down the side of my Dad's armchair. Bingo! I found two coins.

'We need three!' she politely reminded me. *Yes alright!* I thought impatiently.

'I heard that!' Nettie giggled. I giggled too. I had forgotten that Nettie could now read my mind. 'I'm getting quite squished in here! There's not much space with all these thoughts rattling around.'

Next stop was the kitchen and into the larder. The larder was a large walk-in cupboard where we stored all sorts of things. I grabbed three large ice cream sundae dishes from the shelf.

'They're too big!' Nettie corrected me. *Uh-oh, I'd got it wrong again.* I scolded as I felt the frustration rising up.

'Well you didn't say how big they had to be!' I replied defensively.

'Sorry, I need to be more accurate with my words. Okay then. Big enough for the coins to float in,' Nettie added.

I scoured the shelves and saw three small plastic pots my Mum used to put our snacks in. I took a red one, a blue one and a yellow one.

'Excellent! Good work Rubes. Now we need some tomato sauce, some lemon juice and some toothpaste.'

'What on earth...' I started to question, but thought better of it. I had no idea what this was all about, but it was fun. Nettie wasn't going to let me get into trouble. I spoke too soon!

'Who are you talking to, you weirdo!' Jaz poked her head around the door of the larder.

'Don't bite!' Nettie hissed in my ear. 'I'm tidying up. Do you wanna help me?' Nettie prompted me. I repeated Nettie's words to Jaz who was usually nowhere to be seen when help was required.

'You're such a goodie two shoes, Ruby!' Jaz turned on her heel and skipped off humming. *That's an excellent way to get her to leave me alone! Why didn't I think of that before?* I puzzled.

I stretched up to the top shelf to swipe the bottle of tomato sauce. My parents were well prepared. They had back-ups of the essentials like tomato sauce, squash and digestive biscuits in the cupboard. I spied my Mum's shopping basket out of the corner of my eye and started to fill it with the pots and tomato sauce. Next to go in was a bottle of lemon juice. Now I needed to brave the bathroom for the toothpaste.

'I'm right here with you!' Nettie reassuringly squeaked. She sounded a little busy in there.

'You sound like you're doing press ups! What's with all the heavy breathing?' I asked.

'I'm fighting off all these red alerts. Every time you think you're going to get into trouble, you trigger one off! Your brain doesn't even like your sister that much!'

'I love my sisters, but I do usually get into trouble when we argue.' I admitted.

I crept out of the larder and back up the stairs to my bedroom. I didn't want to get stopped and questioned. I grabbed the toothpaste from the bathroom and ran down the corridor to my bedroom. I shut the door and kneeling on my bedroom floor, I tipped out the contents of the shopping basket.

'We need another coin. Do you have a piggy bank?' Nettie asked.

'You won't find anything in there. I had spent all my pocket money on books and stickers. 'But, I know somebody who is rich.' I said getting up. I crept across the corridor to Jemima's room and slowly pushed the door open. I often came in here to try on her clothes when she wasn't here. *Nobody here. The coast is clear!* I felt relieved. I rushed over to her piggy bank and tried to prise it open.

'No, Ruby!' Nettie squeaked. 'She's coming!' I jumped behind the door. As Jemima pushed it open, she created the perfect hiding spot for me. 'Go Rubes!' Nettie squealed so loudly in my head that I could feel my nose start to tickle.

I wiggled my nose and squeezed it with my finger and thumb as if I was about to go underwater. I didn't want to sneeze. Not now! It looked like Jemima was in a hurry as she grabbed her jacket that was slung over a chair. This was no ordinary chair. It was The Chairdrobe — wardrobe chair. Clothes left here were clean. It drove my Mum insane. 'Hang them up! Stop slinging them into a crumpled mess and making more ironing for me!' she would grumble.

'I've got it!' squeaked Nettie as she blocked the sneeze. I wish I could see what she was doing in there. Jemima checked her hair in the mirror and then dashed off. I thought better of taking her coins and remembered the coin I had found at the top of the garden the day we went whale riding with Shoukey and Orchid.

'That's a better idea. Get me out of here!' squeaked Nettie. 'I'm exhausted blocking, stopping and juggling all your worries. You sure are a big thinker! I don't know how you do it, Rubes!' *Neither do I!* I thought.

Safe back in my room, Nettie and I put a towel on the carpet because we couldn't afford to mess that up. We placed the three pots on the towel and filled each one. In the red pot, I squirted tomato sauce. I found the farting noises coming from the air trapped in the bottle hilarious. Nettie, not so much. She rolled her eyes and smiled at me. 'Come on! Lemon juice in the yellow one!' Nettie hurried me along.

'Toothpaste in the blue one!' Nettie sat there watching me fill up the pots.

'Now, before we pop the coins in, I want you to guess which one is going to make the coins sparkle the most she said.

'Is this another test?' It was my turn to roll my eyes.

'It's an experiment to help you to see love in a different way to what you are used to.'

I pulled a face. *How could tomato sauce, lemon juice and toothpaste help me with that?*

'What does love feel like to you, Ruby?' she asked me. Her face was serious and I stopped laughing. It was a serious business. I knew I liked hearing the words 'I love you' because we said it all the time in The Hologram House. When you heard those three little words, it was like magic. You knew you were in the good books. I think that was why I was enjoying lively debates, talking and learning with Nettie. I liked to talk about how I felt. It helped me make sense of everything that would have otherwise been pickled when left floating around inside my head.

'I love the way you listen to me and the way you show me that you understand. You get me!' I looked at the floor, embarrassed. It's not like me. I'm being very gushy today. I had never really thought about or talked about love in this way before. 'How do you like to be loved then?' I asked Nettie, talking to fill the silence and avoid my awkward feelings.

'I feel love constantly,' she said, satisfied. My chest went pang with jealousy. I couldn't imagine what that must feel like. I brought the conversation back to my Mum. 'Is it possible that people can't feel love?' I asked her.

'Love is there, but it may be blocked,' Nettie hinted.

'We give my Mum a lot of gifts and we try to do things that we think will make her happy. I make her cards, I draw her pictures and write her poems. I make her breakfast in bed. I try really hard at school so she will be proud of me. Sometimes she is, but it doesn't last. I made her a birthday cake. I help her around the house, and I pop to the shops when she's run out of stuff. What I mean is—when there is too much darkness, is love enough?' I repeated the question, my mind was frantically searching for the answer. I wondered if there is a way to break out of this horrendous Hologram situation. I refused to give up on it even if they didn't care.

'So which one is it? Which one will make the coins sparkle more brightly?' Nettie brought my attention back to our crazy experiment.

'Urrrm…' I stalled for more time. I didn't want to get it wrong.

'Don't over think it, go with your first thought!' Nettie pleaded.

I decided on toothpaste, because it was a whitening one, and while we waited for the experiment to do its thing we carried on talking.

'Love is enough, Ruby. Fear is the opposite of love. When people are afraid, they try to control things they have no control over. Love is more powerful than fear, but people have to open their hearts to let love in. In life, people suffer—things happen which hurt them. They become bitter and they harden themselves to love. They stop feeling and shut off parts of themselves. They miss the lesson because they're in pain and they prematurely close the door to love. We have to make the effort to choose love instead of fear, even when it's hard.'

'Can you feel love and be scared at the same time?' I asked her.

'Most definitely! All those soft emotions are fragile. That's when you need courage and trust. Trust in yourself.' She made the T sign with her index fingers again. I copied her this time.

We say 'I love you' to one another all the time in my family.' I revealed, wondering if that's a good or bad thing. I groaned inside noticing how I'm forever judging what is good or bad.

'Love is easy to say, but really it's a doing word. Love is in actions and love is freely given. Love is all those little things—an encouraging smile with kind eyes, noticing that you're there. Being pleased to see you and letting you know that you're welcome. Love is spending time together just because. Love doesn't need a plan. Love is remembering to ask 'how are you?' and to hang around long enough to care about the answer. Love can be hard too. Love is telling the truth and having difficult conversations. Love is choosing to be kind instead of right. Love is letting people try it their way, even if it's different to ours. Love allows us to be different without being wrong. Love doesn't have to be right. Love doesn't leave anybody out, it brings everybody together. Love reaches out and holds our hand when we're lonely. Love pulls us up when we fall and says, 'I've got you' and not 'I told you so'. Love sees us and accepts us as we are. Love is the reason we feel wanted. Love shows us that we matter and we're not an afterthought or an inconvenience.'

'Love is lemon juice, toothpaste and tomato sauce?' I tested. 'I love tomato sauce — that much is true!' I joked. Nope. This wasn't a joking matter. I tried again. 'Love is hugging somebody when they cry and helping them when they make a mistake,' I added.

Nettie nodded. 'Yes, Ruby. Love is letting people be who they are and not trying to change them. Love doesn't need us to be perfect. We give love because we want to, not because we expect something in return. Not to control people—to guilt them into doing what we want or to get them to love us back. Love is a choice. Love isn't something you take away when somebody disappoints us or does something we don't like. When people struggle, or suffer, they actually need more love. Love doesn't control. That's fear's job.'

'So, I can love you and feel scared,' I affirmed.

'What is scary about love?' Nettie looked quizzical.

'I'm scared that if I love you, you will find out that I'm really just mean and angry. Then you will go away. You will leave me and that's just too painful to even think about. It's a risk, isn't it—love?' I didn't want her to answer that really.

'You can be afraid of love and choose it anyway,' she replied.

I'm too ashamed to tell Nettie, but I think about the really dark days, when my Dad thinks it's funny to remind my Mum to take her happy pills. I've only ever seen her take vitamins. They're not working, and I don't find that funny! I shake my head. It isn't a joke, it's very sad. Nothing seems to work. It's not like we don't try. The more I think about it, we spend a lot of time trying—the shopping trips, days out at the races, swanky holidays, and cars, the big house, meals out, and the fancy outfits. All the swallowing down of our true feelings to protect her from the truth. I never mean to hurt her. I guess I am sensitive like my Mum.

Tragically, it seems as if that mission is an epic fail. Our attempts to discover the right kind of happy medicine to soothe my Mum's uncontrollable anger were futile. All that stuff gave her temporary joy and fleeting moments of sunshine on her dark days. My Mum looks really pretty when she laughs, but her default setting was cross. It was where she felt most comfortable. Happiness was like a house of cards, it didn't take much before it all came tumbling down.

As I disappeared into a very deep thought hole, one that I visited on a regular basis, I could see clearly all my Mum's efforts were to make me happy too. All the little ways she took care of me had taught me how to do those things for others. I felt duped discovering that this wasn't the way to happiness. I knew that deep down I was miserable too. Maybe Nettie was helping me to see that there was another way. Since I had met Nettie, life was most certainly looking up.

My Mum might never find happiness within herself. Had the anger really eaten it all up and irreversibly blocked her heart? That sobering question brought me back from my busy brain. *I don't want that to happen to me,* I thought about that kind of wretched existence. I definitely didn't want my anger to rob me of my happiness. I didn't want to be a slave to The Hologram House, working harder and harder to maintain the lie. It was a big fun-sucker that chewed up and spat out people's hearts. It destroyed all the real love. I wanted to keep my heart open. I wanted to be brave and stay open to real love.

'The Soul Scroll once told me that *Life isn't to be feared, it was to be lived from the heart, embracing all its raw, messy imperfections and fragility,*' said Nettie. 'Life is fragile and messy, Ruby, and so trying to be neat, tidy, rigid, and tough doesn't work.'

I could see that in my house the fear was so great, it was easier to roll with that, than let go and allow it all to fall away. What would happen if The Hologram slipped through their fingers? What would happen if my Mum chose to live her life in full colour? I knew the chances weren't very high because she had been holding on so tight for so long. It felt too terrifying to step out of her comfort zone. In the black and white world of The Hologram, there was no place for all the colours in between. There was no place for the real messy you that showed up blue on some days and cheery yellow on others. There was no place for angry red or jealous green. In the black and white world, they were numb to it all. There were only two options—right or wrong.

'Ruby! Where are you?' Nettie clicked her fingers to bring me back. I live in my head a lot because I feel safe there.

'I think our experiment is ready,' she said. 'How are you going to fish out those coins and wipe them clean?'

'That's easy! Baby wipes,' I answered. 'These are the most magical invention here on earth. They clean everything!' I started to fish the coins out of the pots and wrap each one in the wipes. When I got to the tomato sauce, I didn't need a wipe. I was quite happy to lick my fingers. As I did the big reveal, I was surprised to see that the lemon juice was more powerful than the toothpaste, but the tomato sauce had won hands down!

'Are you surprised?' Nettie asked.

'I don't think I want to know what is in tomato sauce. I love it so much, but if it cleans dirty coins, then what does it do to me?'

'Well, let's not worry about that too much right now.' Nettie continued. 'The point of the experiment is to show you that some energies you sit in make you more sparkly than others.'

'What, so I can bathe in tomato sauce every day?' I was confused.

'No!' Nettie laughed. 'Think about the energy you sit in every day and what is the best energy to make you sparkle.'

'Oh, I see.' I pulled a face and she filled in the gaps. 'If the energy dulls your shine or doesn't feel good, then what do you need to do?'

'Protect it with my power suit.' Nettie smiled, and I punched the air chuffed to bits that I had fully understood.

'That's it! We can't always choose what energy we are in but we can keep ourselves away from anything that doesn't feel good. People may tell you they love you and maybe their version of love is different to yours,' she finished.

'I most definitely can't choose how my family will be with me.' I nodded, realising that this was a very useful experiment indeed.

'Would you like to come and meet some of the other Wildhearts? Nettie asked. We're holding a gathering at The Nook in a few days and I thought it would be good to meet them. You've already met JB.'

Before I had time to answer, I heard footsteps coming from the other end of the hallway and I quickly stuffed my rucksack in the trunk at the end of my bed. I turned around and Nettie had vanished. *Whoops! I forgot to ask her if the Mermangels had sorted out the wishes.*

CHAPTER 12

A WILD HEART HUDDLE

'Moobs! Did you take my top?' Jemima's head appeared at the door. She knows I hate being called Moobs and I'm not in the mood for any more drama. Luckily, she didn't notice the messy pot coin mess spread on the towel in front of me.

I was about to send her away with a dose of '*Rageful Ruby*', but something I remembered Nettie saying stopped me. I paused to take a breath before I spoke. 'It's in the linen bin,' I replied trying to keep my tone neutral. I expected her to scream the house down and go running to Mum, but she didn't.

'Is it dirty?' she asked clearly irritated. She didn't seem to care how I knew of its whereabouts.

She probably thought I'd taken it without asking or put it there to trick her.

'I don't know. Probably. Do you want to borrow one of mine?' I stayed calm trying to appeal to her better nature.

She sneered, 'What, one of *your* tops?' as if my clothes were cast offs for the recycling bin. I didn't bite.

'It's just an idea. Or we could 'S&B' your top?' I threw her the packet of baby wipes. 'Catch!'

She knows that's funny, but she won't let herself laugh at my joke. We made up S&B together last summer, because we thought it was a good way to make our favourite clothes last just one more day. Spray and Baby wipe was also another secret from my Mum. Firstly, because she hates secrets and secondly, because cleaning clothes with bum wipes and freshly laundering them with air freshener would not have passed her super high laundry levels. I had obviously got the 'right' answer. Perhaps she was going to be kind too and let me be right for once. She snatched the pack of wipes and skipped off to the bathroom to retrieve her top from the musty skids of the linen bin.

'Do you want a hand?' I called after her. It was a token gesture and I crossed my fingers hoping she doesn't hear me.

No answer. I heard her shut her bedroom door, followed by the 'Shhhh-Shhhhh' sounds of her spraying. She was getting busy S&B-ing her outfit. Maybe I was getting better at staying calm and not getting into fights.

I was annoyed that Nettie had gone and our conversation was left unfinished. I was also feeling rather pleased with myself because I had resisted the urge to argue with my sister. Like an itch I didn't scratch, the anger subsided. I hadn't even had to resort to the lip balm. Woo hoo!

In my delight, I decided to make the most of what was left of the evening. I cleared up the pots and returned the stuff from the larder to their rightful homes. I amused myself getting acquainted with the goodies in my rucksack. Every time I pulled a card from the matchbox, I felt reassured. It seemed to have all the answers and had far more understanding than Google. Living between The Hologram and the world inside my head was confusing. That's where I think the doubt came from. I had lost touch with the truth inside of me and at times, it was all too easy to get sucked into the pretence and lies. The force was strong, and it was hard to stay with myself when I was outnumbered. Nobody else could see what I could see. So many people believed in The Hologram and most people were convinced of what a terrible child I was. It was easier and less lonely to give in to the lie instead of being the only one who got it wrong again.

I got ready for bed. 'Luckily, I am strong and gutsy too. I'm very determined and I won't give up. It looks like it may be a battle of wills. Who will win—The Horrendous Hologram or Wilful Wildheart Ruby?' I dramatically role played aloud. With Nettie on my side, I was optimistic. I washed my feet and noticed that it had been a while since I checked the symmetry of my duvet or counted the number of hours of sleep on my alarm clock. The lavender oil was helping me fall asleep quicker and I loved listening to the clear quartz recordings. I put it on my pillow and when the talking stopped, soothing music began. It sounded similar to the classical music we listen to in assembly at school. I loved the gentle sound of the harps and strings. They held me with their soothing notes, a comforting lullaby that melted away the fear in my heart and rocked me safely to sleep.

Earlier, before I had started my nighttime ablutions, I took the rose quartz and put it under my Mum's mattress. Digging deep, I had discovered renewed hope that the energy of this beautiful crystal could help my Mum. *This is it! I really want her to be happy*, were my final thoughts before I peacefully drifted off to sleep.

In the middle of my sweet dreams, I was woken by the sound of Nettie cluttering about behind the curtains. She had knocked over the trinkets and ornaments on the windowsill.

'Pack it in!' I snapped half asleep. Loud noises early in the morning made me grumpy. I glanced at my alarm clock. I had to do a double take. The red digits read 02:00.

'Morning, sleepy head!' she sang, excitedly announcing her news. 'I'm taking you to the Wildheart Huddle!' She pulled back the curtains and blinded me with moonlight.

'Nettieeeeeeee!' I groaned. 'Do you know what the time is?' She really didn't care much for time. She hopped onto my bed and I grabbed the duvet closer to my chin. 'Oh no you don't!' I rolled around and around making myself into a sausage roll with the duvet. 'Huddle schmuddle. Go away!' I mumbled from inside the duvet.

'Oh no you don't, missy!' she giggled, grabbing the end of the duvet and unwrapping me. 'You'll need your rucksack and something warm. After the Huddle, I could really use your help with the Life Library. It's such a mess after Wish Gate. The Mermangels were brilliant, but there's still work to do,' she stood over me gesturing with her hands.

I rubbed my eyes and tried to focus. 'What's a huddle?' I asked. I thought I was ready to meet my Wildheart friends. I wasn't sure what it would be like, but I was sure it would be fun. There would be lots of laughter and no judgment. Nettie was going to let me be me and not punish me or make me feel bad. In fact, if I felt bad, she was going to be there with her pocket tissues to help me mop it up and make sense of it. I wanted to help her with the Life Library as a way to say thank you for everything.

I got myself together, grabbed my rucksack and by the power of heart energy, we were once again transported to the familiarity of The Wilderness. It felt more like home than The Hologram House. It was more beautiful because it was peaceful and calm—there was no stressing, shouting or whirring vacuum noise to disrupt it. 'Where is your crystal, Ruby? Your rose quartz?' Nettie asked.

'I've put it close to my Mum,' I proudly told her and the Wildhearts who stood in front of me with their wide eyes gazing back at me. We were all gathered round closely in a circle. I guess this is what you would call a huddle. 'I put it under her mattress so she can feel the loving vibes.' I was visibly chuffed to bits and relieved all at the same time.

Judging by the looks on their faces, the rest of the group seemed to think this was a bad idea. Now, I could feel my cheeks blushing and I started to wrack my brain wondering what on earth I had done wrong this time. It looked like I'd made a huge mistake.

'It feels like you want to help your Mum,' Nettie observed.

'Well, I've tried all the ways I can to love her and her heart must be blocked. So, I thought the crystal could work its magic,' I defended my position.

'You're very kind, Ruby.' All the other Wildhearts were nodding and smiling, but I could tell that something was off. They wouldn't look at me in the eye for very long. They were fixated on Nettie, waiting for her to spill the beans. 'Is that it, or are you trying to protect yourself?' she asked.

'Are you trying to protect yourself from the terrifying anger and the punishments?'

'I certainly don't like the anger or the scary punishments. I do love my Mum though, and I want her to be happy.' I thought aloud. 'I guess I want our family to be different. My Mum is in charge, so I figured if she was happy, then it would make a big difference … for the better …' my voice trailed off as I started to question my motives.

'Wanting the best for the people you love is truly kind, but nothing will change unless the other people in your family change too. Families are a team. They're all on the same side, but everybody is responsible for their own happiness. How can you possibly know the lessons your Mum needs to learn to unlock her heart again?' she asked me, tilting her head to one side.

'I don't.' I looked at the floor and felt cross with myself. I'd forgotten my crystal *and* I'd messed it all up. The horrid feeling sat heavy in my tummy and I sank into the familiar feeling of being the wrong one. It was too much for a first meeting, I didn't even know their names. My legs were shaking. They were getting ready to run away.

'I do understand. Most of your ideas and intentions come from love, Ruby. I know you care, but what is right for you may not be right for your Mum. Only she knows that, and she has to make her own choices,' she finished.

The other children looked down at the ground. One by one their heads fell like dominoes and the atmosphere in the huddle became thick and intense. It was as if they too had tried to help their families and learnt that it was not possible. My brain had started to fire up the quiz master and I could tell it wanted to find out more about them. My questions were answered as Nettie asked each one of us to step forward and introduce ourselves. She told us to share something we loved and something we didn't like so much. My mind was occupied. The running feeling had gone, and I stayed put.

'Hi! I'm Delta and I love fireflies and hate the rain.' Going first means you get it over and done with. Then you can enjoy listening to what everybody else is saying without having your turn hanging over you. Delta stepped back and didn't look bothered at all.

I panicked slightly, as I didn't have time to perfect my answer. So I said the first thing that popped into my head, 'Hi I'm Ruby and I love cheese, and I hate liars.' I cringed. *My body looked apologetic, like it was taking up too much space in the circle. Why couldn't I think of something cool to say*? the scolding parent voice piped up again.

A little laugh rippled through the group. There were ten of us—including me—all huddled together surrounded by the beautiful backdrop of The Wilderness. The bandstand welcomed the night with twinkling fairy lights. There was no choir tonight. The peaceful silence held the rolling hills that made silhouettes against the pink sky. The twilight was neither dark nor light. It was neither right or wrong.

'None of us like lies,' Nettie responded to my introduction. 'It's a very strong trait in Wildhearts. We speak the truth even when our voice shakes. Often, it can get us into trouble, but we believe so hard in doing the right thing that it feels wrong not to speak up.'

I noticed that we were standing close to the entrance of The Nook and inches away, the leafy woodland went on for miles. That uncomfortable feeling had flooded my body again, but I tried not to fight it or make it wrong. I let it be. I rested my hand over my heart, inhaling deeply. The anticipation that something else could go wrong hung in the air. I mentally beat myself up. I felt embarrassed and stupid for not being more original. I'm so out of sorts when I'm unprepared. I expect they'll all be thinking that I'm a real weirdo.

Come on, Ruby, I reminded myself. *You're here to meet people and have fun. Try again*!

I smiled at the girl next to me, hoping she would be my new friend. She smiled back and the icky feeling shrank. It was her turn next. She cautiously stepped forward. 'Hi! I'm Robyn!' her voice wobbled. 'I love rabbits and I don't really like angry people and loud noises.' She shuffled back, her head bowed.

'Hi, I'm Gabe and I hate going to sleep but I love my bed.' His voice was strong and sensible. When he stepped back, I could see that he was the tallest in the group. *Wow! His bed must be giant sized!* I reflected on how I also love the cosy squishiness of my bed, but how tricky night times could be.

My mind chattered on, *I love the pitter-patter of rainy Saturdays, when I'm tucked up safely indoors reading. I should have said I love books instead of cheese*, I corrected myself. Then I started to worry that Robyn wouldn't like me if she found out I was so angry. *Maybe we don't have anything in common—I'm more of a cat person,'* I thought protecting myself from being disliked.

'I'm India. I love yoga and hate meat,' she confidently boomed, with emphasis on *hate*. Phew, luckily, I hadn't yet mentioned my love of sausages. I noticed India was wearing a long, beaded necklace with a crystal pendant. It matched her turquoise t-shirt that looked like her Mum had put on a hot wash—all the colours had run together. My Mum does that when a rogue red sock sneaks into the white wash. She'll be less angry when she discovers that she's not actually tarnishing her domestic Goddess persona and is fashionably on trend. It's called tie-dye, apparently.

'Hey everyone! I'm Harri!' he did an awkward wave with flimsy wrists, his cute dimples beaming from ear to ear. 'I love to dance and I hate football.' *I know how he feels.*

'Well, I love all sports, especially football and I hate being told off. My name is Freddie.' I looked at Harri who was still beaming and didn't appear to be bothered by Freddie's opposing taste. *I guess it must be okay to like different things.*

'Thank you, Freddie. Thank you everybody. Now, I thought we'd have a go at flexing our intuition muscles. It's time for a game!' Nettie clapped her hands to get our attention. I managed to switch off my boggled mind long enough to listen.

'So, we'll use my rose quartz for this.' She took the small crystal and placed it in the middle of the circle. I followed her instructions. It sounded straightforward enough. It was a game of hunt the crystal without using your eyes or a blindfold. Basically, the designated crystal hunter would leave the circle, one of the people left in the circle would hide the crystal in their hands. Then the crystal hunter would return to the circle and guess who was holding the crystal. I wasn't sure I understood how it was going to work, but it was a bit like when my Dad put both his hands behind his back and asks me to guess in which hand he was hiding a sweet or a coin. I was quite good at that.

JB offered to go first and he left the circle. He wondered off behind a tree and once he was out of sight, Nettie pointed at India. India confidently retrieved the crystal from the centre of the circle and returned to her place. Nettie signalled for us all to watch her as she demonstrated what to do next. She crossed her legs, clasped her hands together and brought them to rest gently in her lap. We all did the same, including India, who was hiding the crystal between her palms.

'Okay, JB! We're ready for you,' Nettie called towards trees.

JB ambled back to the circle. When he reached the middle, he took off his shoes and planted his feet firmly on the grass. He closed his eyes and took three deep breaths. We watched him with intense fascination. There was no noise, but you could feel the energy all around. JB opened his eyes, and purposefully directed his feet at me. He spent a few moments scanning me like a loaf of bread at the supermarket checkout. *Beep Beep*! He gradually made his way around the circle. When he arrived back where he started, he took another deep breath in. He was really milking it, and the not knowing suspense was killing me. Finally, he pointed to India!

Incredible! How did he do that? India was laughing as she showed him the crystal in her hand. 'Well done! How did you do that JB?' she asked.

He shrugged. 'Urrm. I'm listening to my body and letting it go where it wants to. I was letting it lead the way. I take my time. I trust myself. I kind of get an inkling of where to go.' He tries to share his experience with us.

I pulled a face. *What is this inkling? How can your body know where to go? Surely you have a one in ten chance of guessing correctly? It's like a multiple choice when you don't know the answer!* I thought.

The others were all making the T sign with their index fingers. I swapped the face for T fingers and felt a bit better. If I was going to get the hang of this trusting, I needed to get the moves right.

'It helps to be relaxed and not over think it,' Nettie added. 'As does grounding your energy—taking it out of your head and into your body. That's why JB took his shoes off and let his feet touch the earth. That's how your intuition works. It's the part of you that knows before you know, but you need to be connected to it instead of the one that makes your mind busy with all the nasty worries.'

'Can you tell from our faces if it's us?' asked another girl. I can't remember her name. I noticed her plaits were wonky but she was asking all the smart questions. I wanted to restyle them.

'No, Aurora! Not that I'm aware of.' JB turned to Nettie, who continued explaining. 'We're mentally scanning each other all the time. We don't realise that we're sending out messages without saying a single word. In fact, talking is only seven per cent of our communication with one another.'

Intrigued and true to Wildheart form, we were all leaning forward to geek out on the new facts. I thought about my face pulling and joked to myself that the frowning and grimacing had to be a dead giveaway. I also felt quietly confident that I was over-qualified and would nail this game. I can pre-empt my Mum's moods and unspoken requests in a heartbeat. I also know my Dad's look of contempt, the one which says, 'You've gone too far!' I was less nervous about it when it was my turn and a little thankful that my family had taught me something useful for a change.

'What sort of messages?' asked wonkily plaited Aurora. I sat on my hands. What is wrong with me? I must have still been feeling a little worried because I want to de-wonkify them.

'Blinking too much indicates we might be nervous. So does licking or biting our lips. If we play with our hair or touch our faces, we're unsure. When we fold our arms, we're protecting ourselves.' I thought about how I bowed my head and held onto my ears when my Mum's angry hands strike, or how I swerved my body away from my Dad, to avoid a wallop.

'Notice how your feet are in the circle. Are they pointing towards the centre or at somebody else's?

Is your body open or closed? Is your body inviting people to approach you—that's open. Or are you closed off from connecting with others? I think sometimes we aren't aware that we are making ourselves unavailable to others with the way we hold ourselves.

'Do you hold your body up or hunch over? How do you walk?' Nettie strutted around the circle as if she was on a catwalk as she fired questions at us. We all looked down at our feet and then up again, pushing our shoulders back. Aurora flicked her plaits over her shoulders and Harri looked like he'd just received a medal. You could tell he was a dancer because of the way he stood. He had ten-to-two feet, his feet have high arches and they turn outwards.

'Keep your heads up! Look ahead! Show me what you've got! That's it—give it some swagger!' Nettie encouraged playfully. I could see Robyn found this difficult. She had shoved her hands in her skirt pockets. Meanwhile, India jangled her beady bracelets up her arm as she adjusted her posture. She rested back on her left leg and pointed her other foot to the right. Her hands were on her hips which is exactly the stance I adopt when I've been woken up. I'd fly down the stairs and stand there.

'Why do you have to make so much noise?' I tell my family, but they laugh at me and carry on.

'Well done, India! That's a Power Pose. Notice what you're thinking and how you're feeling inside. Your body will reflect that,' Nettie stood there admiring our efforts.

Freddie and JB were getting rather noisy. They were messing about pretending to walk sideways like crabs and knocking into one another. Delta glared at them, rather bored by it all. She folded her arms across her body. Her mouth was clamped tight shut as if she wasn't going to indulge in such ridiculousness.

'You know what would be a fun experiment and excellent practice for all of you when you leave here? You could make it your goal to watch people when they are not talking. See if you can guess how they might be feeling from their facial expressions.'

We nodded eagerly. I didn't feel like this when Mrs Barnes gave us homework. 'I also want you to be more aware of how you walk, stand, and hold your body. Smiles automatically put people at ease—the person giving the smile and the person receiving it. Smiling is the universal sign for kindness.' she concluded. Instantly, we all smiled at each other and then burst into laughter. The mood of the group was relaxed and light-hearted. I noticed how it was so different from being at school or even when we had guests visit The Hologram House. This was a new way of socialising for me. The tension was replaced with fun. I guess it was easier to have fun when there was nobody to impress.

'Anybody else want to try?' Nettie asked. Aurora guessed the first time, her plaits certainly didn't affect her performance. Next up was Gabe. As he left the circle, Nettie pointed to me. It's my turn to be the keeper of the crystal. I secretly hoped I didn't mess it up. Gabe had a different technique to the others. He came to the edge of the circle and without making eye contact, stood in front of each one of us with his eyes closed. When he had finished, he opened his eyes and said to Nettie, 'Is it, Ruby?'

Yay! We all clapped and talked about why he had chosen to do it differently. Gabe said that he wanted to be closer so he could feel the energy of the crystal.

'It's great you're all working out the best way for you. There is no right way to do it. There are lots of different ways!' Nettie told us. My shoulders dropped. 'It's trial and error. It's so much fun finding out. You all have super strong intuition. Most Wildhearts do!'

CHAPTER 13

THE HEARTFELT WELCOME

'When we're reading body language or other people's auras, it's important that we've protected ours. We're very sensitive and easily pick up other people's feelings,' Nettie reminded us.

'How can you really feel somebody else's feelings?' I asked. Some days I feel so heavy with emotion. I have questioned before if it's all mine, but I want to understand more.

'When you're sensitive, you're open to all energies around you. Some people are affected by the weather and the change of seasons.' Nettie explains.

'I love the rain,' I said glancing sideways at Delta who frowned.

Nettie carried on, 'You could walk into a room and sense the mood of the people in it. It's like their feelings stick to you like Velcro or you absorb them like a sponge. You could be queuing in a shop and all of a sudden feel a pang of anger or sadness which could be from the person standing next to you. Over time you'll learn to work out what belongs to you and what belongs to others. That's why we must protect our energy Ruby, because we get tired feeling everybody else's feelings, and it also makes it hard to be with our own.'

'Eeek! I didn't put my power suit on today,' I confessed to the group. 'Mind you, it was 2:00 am when I left my bedroom and I was moonflower powered here with bed hair and eye bogies.' I added.

'Oh, I used to do that,' Aurora said, yanking on her left plait so it was finally aligned with the right one. I felt my shoulders drop some more. 'I find it helps if you do it while you're cleaning your teeth or when you're getting dressed. It's just an extra layer of clothing; another part of your morning routine.'

'I step into a bubble,' Freddie chipped in. 'I imagine my bubble closing around me as I step outside of my front door.'

'That's a good idea,' says a wide-eyed little boy with long hair. 'What do you do, Kam?' Nettie asked him.

'When I brush my hair in the mirror, I pretend to make a rainbow like this,' he made an arc with his hands in the air over his head. 'I can see all the colours in my mind and it's so cool.' he proudly shared.

'I'm with Ruby,' said Aurora. 'I have a pink power suit and I put it on like this. She started to sing, 'I'm zipping up my energy to keep me safe and strong, I'm zipping up my energy to protect me all day long.' As she sang, she pretended to step into her power suit, zipping herself all the way from her feet to the top of her head.

Nettie cleared her throat and everybody looked at her. 'While we're all here I'd like us to properly welcome Ruby. She has been working hard to uncover new lessons and facing some big scary fears. She's making big strides and doing so well.' The Wildhearts clapped. I blushed crimson, my freckles were on fire.

'Ruby,' she turned to face me and took both my hands. 'We have an extra special tradition to welcome all new Wildhearts to The Wilderness.

We're delighted to have you here with us. Please can we welcome your beautiful heart?'

Before I had time to reply, she whispered, 'Go on now!' and ushered me into the middle of the circle. The others drew closer, and I waited for the worries to start. As I stood there looking at all the happy faces around me, I realised it wasn't awful at all. I was slightly self-conscious, but the smiles were definitely helping.

Nettie held a selenite wand in one hand. It was about four times the size of the baby one she had gifted me. She asked the others to close their eyes and beam heart energy to me. She stretched her other hand up to the sky. She looked like a warrior, as she began, 'We're so glad you're here, Ruby. We welcome you into our family of Wildhearts and we want to share our wonderful home The Wilderness with you. We send Ruby pure heart energy to wash away her bad feelings. For any bad feelings she may have about being who she truly is. Any mistakes she has made, she is simply learning. She has learnt so much and her heart, body, and mind are full of wisdom so she can help others. We give Ruby the courage to face her fears and trust that all her Wildheart experiences are to strengthen and help her. We wrap her in an invisible cloak of loving kindness to hold her tight.' She swirled the wand around over her head.

'Let's light her up!' Nettie exclaimed. All the Wildhearts were holding moonflowers and each one was directed towards me. I felt my chest expanding as the moonflowers shone together. I felt as if I was getting bigger. The light was beautiful, making rainbows as it bounced off Nettie's crystal wand.

'Hold out your hands and allow our messages of hope in. They will stay with you and soothe you when you feel lost or life gets tricky.' said Nettie.

The purple petals of hope are handed to me one by one and each child softly spoke words of comfort as their eyes met mine with a smile.

'Appreciation for all that you are and all that you're becoming. Thank you, Ruby.' The first flower lay in my cupped hands.

'Acceptance for every single part of you, no matter what. Thank you, Ruby.' Another flower brushed my palm.

'Comfort for times of loneliness and sorrow. May it hold you in a big warm hug. Thank you, Ruby.' I bit my lip as Freddie handed me the glowing petals.

'Validation for all your experiences, your hurty bits, and your struggle. Your truth is real, we hear it and we believe you. Thank you, Ruby.'

I took a big gulp of air, my shoulders dropped, another flower fell.

'Understanding for your rage, your anger, for all your mistakes, your bad moods, your cruel words. Right your own wrongs and forgive yourself. Thank you, Ruby.'

I felt a hot flush of shame coursed through my body. The flowers turned blurry through the tears.

'Encouragement for when it feels hard and you want to give up. May your fiery energy take you to where you need to go. Thank you, Ruby.'

My bottom lip quivered.

'Positivity when you've forgotten who you are and what great things you're capable of. Thank you, Ruby.'

I tried to smile back at JB. A tear slid down my freckly face.

'Protection for your fear and when you're surrounded by darkness. May your light shine brighter than the stars. Thank you, Ruby.' Kam told me stumbling back.

And so they fell, each tiny flower into my hands, quenching my thirsty soul. Aurora stepped forward. 'Courage to be different and uniquely you. May you always remember who you are and be true to that. Thank you, Ruby.' She stepped back, her plaits were in perfect alignment.

Then it was Nettie's turn. She came forward and handed me a tissue, 'LOVE. LOVE. LOVE. So much love for you, Ruby. You are always loved. We love you just as you are.' She stayed close.

I had never enjoyed an early morning, but this one was different. This morning's sunrise was overflowing with kind and uplifting words. My hands were full of moonflowers. The emotions were overwhelming. I started to cry. Nettie put her hands underneath mine to support my sadness. 'Let them fall,' she said. 'Let them wash it all away.'

We all went and sat on the grass. We were still enjoying our morning silence together when Nettie left to go and fetch some much needed refreshments. It wasn't an awkward silence, like the one at our kitchen table. I usually talk to fill silences, but this one was like a squishy beanbag that you could rest in.

'Iced rose tea,' Nettie appeared holding a tray of goblets. She handed one to each of us. They were filled with pink liquid and the odd floating petal. 'Well done. That was amazing. To you!'

congratulated Nettie. We brought our cups together and toasted. 'To all the Wildhearts! Cheers!' Clink. Smile. Clink, Smile, clink, clink, clink. The birds were firing up their morning chorus. They had competition—the choir was arriving at the bandstand. The fairy lights were now replaced by the sun in the sky.

'Thank you,' I blew my nose, feeling raw after all the crying. I looked into my goblet and thought it was a bit strange to be drinking flowers. It tasted rather nice. An unexpected sob juddered through my little body. Nobody tried to stop me or distract me from crying. They didn't ignore me either. They were close by, letting me be what I needed to be. I was so grateful not to have to dig deep and find the energy to be *'Show Ruby'!* I didn't have the energy for it.

'When I first came here, I was so angry that I felt like my head would pop,' Aurora revealed. 'You know it's all fading when you have a good cry.'

'Me too,' confirmed Freddie. Kam and the others were nodding too. 'What about you, Robyn?' Nettie asked.

'I don't get angry,' she said fiddling with the bottom of her bronze goblet.

'What, nothing makes you mad or annoys you?' asked Kam who was picking all the petals out of his tea and wiping them on the grass.

'I seem to cry more than get angry when people upset me.' Robyn clarified.

'What, you don't feel like you want to shout at them or get them back?' Kam kept on the pressure with his questions. Wildhearts would make such excellent FBI Agents or Detectives with their ninja questioning skills.

'Of course, I get them back, but they don't know it's me.' Robyn bit her lip and frowned. She couldn't decide if it was a good idea to share with the others or not.

'Sneaky smarts! What do you do to get them back?' asked Kam looking more interested in the way the conversation was heading.

'The Karma fairies take care of that.' Gabe interjected. 'The Karma fairies are the only people who get to decide who gets payback.'

India backed him up, 'In the Gold Books, some life lessons are payback. What you give out you get back. If you spend your life being a bully, then you will receive the same sort of cruelty at some point. You don't get to decide when, with whom, and how it happens. The Karma fairies do.'

'It works the other way too!' Gabe led the conversation again, slightly put out that India was stealing his five minutes of fame. 'What you put out you get back. So, Freddie here likes to make people laugh, and he will get joy back in his life, but not necessarily from the people he gave it too originally.'

'My Dad is a big old bully, so he's got it coming to him.' Delta remarked bitterly. She still hadn't uncrossed her arms. I wondered if they were glued together. 'He's quite nice sometimes ...' she threw in as an afterthought, worried she'd taken it too far.

India started up again, 'Sadly, there are meanies in this world, but I don't think they are born mean. I believe their Karma is the pain and misery they carry inside of them every day. We're born to love and connect with one another, not to be cruel and heartless. Imagine living your whole life not being able to truly love and connect to others. That is punishment enough, isn't it?'

'People who have hurt you will feel that hurt too and it goes in the Gold Book as a lesson learnt. So there is no need for you to take revenge,' Nettie reminded us. 'Acknowledge the anger, then let it go. Leave it to the Karma Fairies. The best thing you can do is get on and live a happy life. Don't give that person power over you.'

You could hear the cogs turning, as we all frantically thought about the good, the bad and the ugly. I reckon my Mum and I are probably equal. I'm no angel that's for sure. I can remember the time I locked my little sister in Snowy's shed and made her cry. My toes curl over thinking about it and I hope that one day she will forgive me.

'I can't cry.' Kam said totally railroading the Karma conversation. It felt like he wanted to carry on our conversation from before. There were things he needed to say.

'You can borrow some of my tears,' I offered.

'I think you get more attention when you cry,' Robyn divulged.

'If you're a girl!' Kam became quite animated. 'Otherwise you get teased. I don't want them to see me crying. I don't want them to think they have upset me. I have to be tough.' He flexed his muscles like a body builder. I wanted to laugh but at the same time, I thought it was sad. I couldn't imagine being a boy and not being able to cry.

'So you *do* cry then?' said Robyn.

'And you get angry but you sneaky sneak it away so nobody knows!' Kam retorted.

'This is an interesting conversation,' remarked Nettie. 'Boys can't cry because they have to be tough. Girls cry to get more attention. Wow, guys, I'm not sure that's what your tears are for. I think crying is ...'

'Wouldn't you rather be noticed for who you are instead of when you're feeling sad?' Harri interrupted. 'At school, I'm known as the boy who doesn't play football and that's kind of annoying because being a boy *and* a good dancer isn't a combo that counts for very much.'

Delta sneered, 'You really care about what they think? Big deal! Who cares?' I'm not sure her words match what her body is saying. She lifted her folded arms up and then put them back on her chest forcefully. Yep, they most definitely are glued.

'They bully me, and it hurts,' Harri said indignantly. He put his hands over his tummy, clearly upset by Delta's cold heartedness.

'You can't be who other people want you to be. You can only be yourself.' Gabe showed us how wise he was and diffused the tension. 'Nettie taught me to put the horrible words on an imaginary boomerang and visualise them being sent back to where they came from.'

‘Don’t let them in your heart!’ India proclaimed as she protectively placed her hands to her chest.

‘Other people need you to be a certain way, so that they can feel okay. They want you to be okay, ‘cos they love you ... but when you do stuff that makes them feel afraid or uncomfortable, forget it. They want to change you. Shut you down.’ JB sounded like he was speaking from experience.

‘That’s why I like coming here,’ said Kam. ‘You can be who you are, feel what you like, and people understand. When you feel happy and free to be you, you do less stupid stuff.’

That’s all I want—a little understanding. My family doesn’t get it at all.’ complained Aurora.

‘I feel you!’ I said to Aurora. ‘It makes me want to scream.’

I turned to JB. ‘It takes effort to pretend and push down all the unacceptable feelings. You know, hold them all in!’

‘Like farts!’ Freddie burst into laughter. I sniggered which unexpectedly turned into a snort.

‘Freddie!’ Gabe’s serious voice was like a stern parent. Freddie didn’t care and he wasn’t listening, he started making fart noises with his mouth. I couldn’t control my laughter. I held my tummy and my shoulders went up and down. It felt good to laugh out loud after all that crying.

‘Let the wind be free!’ India was joining in now and had caught the giggles. Robyn blushed putting her hand over her mouth, as if farting was forbidden. I’m not sure it could be even if we wanted it to! Harri was sniggering and poking his tongue out at Freddie.

‘Right, you lovely lot!’ Nettie got to her feet. ‘This is fun, but I have work to do. The Life Library needs a make-over. Can I get some helpers please?’ she requested. ‘I’ll help!’ Aurora, Harri and Kam all chorused at once over their snorting-giggling-farting noises. ‘Count me out,’ said Delta flatly. She didn’t seem to want to get involved. It was so hard to read her. India fiddled with her beads and looked down.

‘I’ve got footy!’ Freddie jumped up and returned his empty goblet back to the tray. As he bent down, JB blew a raspberry. ‘Oops! Pardon me!’ said Freddie, putting on a posh voice. ‘That flowery water really doesn’t agree with me!’

CHAPTER 14

THE SURPRISE UNDERSTANDING

Nettie wasn't wrong! The Life Library was unrecognisable and the mess made me feel a little queasy. The table in the middle of the room was covered in stacks of unfiled books. The tall rainbow towers made a buzzing sound, as if the wishes couldn't wait a minute longer. I wanted to know what the other Wildhearts were wishing for. Did we all want the same thing? Were there enough wishes to go around?

'We're over here!' cried a voice from behind the multi-coloured mountains. The spine of each book was adorned with intricate calligraphy that spelt out each Wildheart's name. The dazzling gold leaf made it impossible to read the names. I wondered if I knew any of them.

'Watch where you're going!' The Soul Scroll's Feather danced around the books trying not to knock them over. In a corner, the Mermangels had taken charge with a simple production line. It reminded me of pretend play Librarian days. I watched them opening and shutting the books before methodically filing them away. They didn't seem overwhelmed or distracted by the sheer number of them.

Open. Shut. File. Open. Shut. File. Heads down, focussed and determined. It was hypnotic. I recognised the smell of the Mermangels: vanilla essence and saltwater took me back to the Selenite Caves. Today, they were wearing shoes. Their silvery scaly tails were replaced with human legs and their long eye lashes fluttered with concentration. Open. Shut. File. Nothing was going to stop them from granting wishes to their rightful makers. Open. Shut. File. Open. Shut. File. Open. Shut. File. Their repeated actions created a rhythmic beat. I could feel its energy motivating them to finish the task at hand. I saw Starry but her head was lost in the books and she couldn't see me.

'We have to keep filing because another batch of books is due in very soon,' announced The Soul Scroll as he frantically passed one to Kam. 'Thanks,

Scrowlie!' he cheekily christened The Soul Scroll. I thought it was daring to do so. He was like royalty: the speaker of all truth, the interpreter of dreams and carrier of profound wisdom.

Kam grimaced and it looked like he was doubting his over-familiar gesture, but The Soul Scroll wasn't fazed. *I like that*, he started to write. *My job is serious, but I like to have fun too. Thanks, Kam*. He drew a smiley face. Kam looked chuffed to bits and basked in the praise.

He continued, *I have the same job as the newspapers and television, but they aren't feeding young brains with information that grows and expands them. Your imaginations are nourished by creativity, play and wonder. They are muddying your impressionable minds with lies and negativity. Your minds are full of fear and worries. All the positivity and child-like innocence are brainwashed out of you.*

Kam read the words and looked puzzled. Nettie helpfully summarized, 'Be careful what you feed your mind with. Your brain is always listening, and it believes what you tell it is true. Do you guys spend a lot of time staring at your screens?'

'I don't watch the news.' Harri declared. 'It's boring and sad. When I see people sick and dying, I want to cry. I prefer to listen to music. I don't want to hear about terrorism and boring politics. My dad worries about his job and those scary images and stories stay with me for days.'

'I like it when old people get a letter from the Queen. Can you imagine having a 100 th birthday?' Aurora continued to talk very quickly about how much old people smell and how they might like something other than lavender soap. Her brain is as fast and as curious as mine, but there is no filter for her stream of questions. Yes, that was it! Poor Aurora! Her thought filter was broken. Thoughts literally went straight from her brain and poured out of her mouth at a gazillion miles per hour. I mentally zipped up my power suit to protect myself from her thought shower. Having too many of my own thoughts was more than enough.

'I love to read books about magic with happy endings,' Harri talked over her. Another one of my Dad's sayings springs to mind 'She could talk her way out of a paper bag!' I chuckled. It's funny to see somebody else being like that. I'm usually the one who gets told off for talking too much and at the wrong times. Aurora didn't stop for breath, and Harri looked triumphant. He's actually managed to make his point. I wondered if we could help Aurora repair her filter. I don't think they sell them online, but I make a note to investigate later. It's quite possible that we were both born without one.

'Why can't you magic them?' I asked, bringing everybody back to the challenge at hand. My mega detective brain was automatically assessing what was possible, so I could come up with a master plan. It loves to sniff out problems, create them—sometimes when there aren't any—or troubleshoot other people's. My brain really does want to help but it also wants to be in control. I feel very scared when I'm not in charge of what is happening. I have to trust other people to do what they say they're going to do. In my experience, other people will and do disappoint.

'Use heart energy to speed it up!' I suggested.

'We can't by-pass the important work, Ruby. We have to check that the wisher really believes their wish will come true. That's why we roped in the Mermangels. Their super high levels of sensitivity mean they can weed out doubters. As the Rainbow Books fall from the shoot, we have to see if they've been stamped by a Mermangel. All the ones with a B stamped on the inside cover are ready to be granted. They go on these shelves here. The ones without a B— the wobbly wishes, are thrown into The Desire Pit until the next Moon cycle. Doubt is like a butterfly you can't catch. It flutters in your mind, distracting you from the truth.' Nettie told me. 'When your brain gets tired and stressed it slows down. Stay with your truth, what feels right for you. It's all about how you feel.'

'I doubt myself every time.' I reluctantly admitted. 'I don't believe it will happen for me. I have to find evidence and see it to believe it.'

Aurora peered into The Desire Pit. It was a hole in the corner of the Life Library that was deceptively deep. As Aurora spoke, her voice echoed deep into the bowels of the earth. 'There's nothing in there ... there ... there ... Are you granting all the wishes ... wishes ... wishes?'

Before Aurora could crank up her train of thought, Scrowlie stepped in, *It's a temporary vault that holds the wishes until the next New Moon. If the wisher has given up on the wish, it falls into this bottomless pit where the flames of desire burn it to ashes. However, if the wisher is still hopeful, the flames destroy the doubt and spark off new belief. With no doubt and strong belief, it's still possible the wish can be granted.*

Wow! My mind was boggled. I floated off into my own little world to make sense of it all. Aurora continued to say all her thoughts out loud. She was annoying me now. Is this my payback for what my family has to suffer when my mouth goes into overdrive? I wonder what it's like for them to be met by my stream of babble that constantly reminds them of all the things they are trying to forget.

Kam opened the book he had been given and scanned the inside front cover. 'It has a B!' he said rushing to file it away like an untrained puppy. His over-enthusiasm knocked the edge of the table, and suddenly there were books everywhere. I was helpless as I watched the tallest tower of books topple in slow motion to the ground.

Whilst Kam and the others scrambled to put the books back, I was still trying to work out the filing system. I found it remarkable that nobody told Kam off. He was allowed to make a mistake and put it right without being reminded. 'What do you say?' is definitely a stock favourite phrase in The Hologram House. Kam seemed genuinely sorry and without prompting said so gracefully and sincerely.

'How?! How can you tell if the wisher still believes or not?' I continued with my obsessive line of questioning. I scratched my head, unsure that it was possible to know what was true for somebody else.

Scrowlie continued, *If you believe, you have to feel something one million per cent with all your heart and soul, even when there's no evidence. This is easier for some and really tricky for others. You don't have to see something to believe it. If there's any doubt, you don't fully believe. The Mermangels are skilled at reading each Wildheart's energy. They can use their strong heart energy to tune in to the emotion. So, if a Wildheart's energy vibrates high and strong, they believe. Whereas, uncertainty has a much lower vibration.*

'Worry has a low vibration too,' said Aurora joining in.

'It does!' said Nettie impressed with Aurora's knowledge. 'Although worriers can go to places in their heads that other people only dream about. They are deep thinkers with amazing imaginations. That's why it's so important that you all learn how to use your imaginations to create and not to terrify yourselves!'

And fear, guilt and shame, Scrowlie seized the moment before Aurora could pipe up again. *No good can come of such low vibrations when you're making a wish. If you think you don't deserve it, or it won't happen for you – you're afraid it won't come true, it won't. The power is in your hands because you get to choose what to believe and how hard. You can believe whatever you like. Nobody can tell you what to believe. They are your thoughts, it's your mind. Nobody has access to that. Isn't that a wonderful thing?*

I was impressed by the super powers of the Mermangels. Nettie had previously explained to me that the Mermangels are aqualess beings. That means they have a tail when they get wet and legs when they're dry. They have the healing guidance of an angel and the powers of a mermaid. Who knew that a mermaid could boil and freeze water? Their energetic sensitivity and empathy are an exact match for the Wildhearts who struggle in the real world to manage these gifts.

'Tell us your wish, Ruby,' Nettie invited me to share.

'I wish that my Mum was happy,' I blurted.

'No. A wish for you. That's very sweet, Ruby. Your Mum has to make her own wishes,' Nettie coaxed.

'Okay!' I blushed. I had got it wrong again. I quickly searched around in my mind for an answer.

Nothing. 'It is for me,' I protested. 'If my Mum is happy, then I am too.'

'No. A wish for you,' Nettie repeated. 'We can't make wishes for others.' She placed her hand on her heart and nodded towards me.

I followed her lead and no sooner had I put my hand over my heart, the words flew out of my mouth, 'I wish I could be, Ruby. I want to be me without having to think too hard about it.'

'Me too,' echoed Harri. 'When you aren't like the other boys, they tease you and it's hard to be different. You want to keep it a secret to protect yourself.'

Nettie nodded. 'Okay, and do you believe that's possible, young lady?' she pretended to hold a microphone in her hand as if she was interviewing me.

'I'm not sure,' I giggled. I love the way she makes the tricky stuff funny. It helps to laugh.

'What are your choices?' she playfully put the pretend microphone up to my mouth again.

'I could find more friends who get me or try harder for people to like me. I could be less annoying.' I went along with the pretending and leant over to talk into the invisible microphone.

'How do you think you annoy people?' she asked.

'When I tell the truth, people get mad. They want to silence my voice. I've been taught that it's better to tell the truth than to get caught in a lie. Lies break trust, but they lie all the time,' I trailed off.

'I don't want to tell the truth about my dancing,' Harri mumbled. He looked ashamed that he might have unknowingly been lying. Wildhearts hate dishonesty.

'I get it, Harri,' I wanted to show him I was on his side. 'You're not deceitful, but you want to protect yourself from the mean bullies who won't stop teasing you.' I could see he was having icky feelings and I immediately wanted to take them away.

'Some people are threatened by that. It takes courage to swim against the tide,' Nettie said.

'It's crazy to think that by being yourself, you could somehow drive people away or make them horrible to you,' I questioned the logic of that.

Scrowlie was on standby with his words of wisdom, *You can't make people do or say things. That is their choice.*

'Why do my family lie about who they are then? Why do they pretend to be perfect, when we're no different from any other family?' I asked, secretly pleased that it wasn't my fault. 'What are they protecting themselves from?'

The words fell on the page. *They feel ashamed of their flaws, but flaws are what make us human. Sometimes the quirkiest things about us are what make us who we are! We're all different in our own way and we're meant to be. Everybody has their own brand of specialness, but nobody is more special than another.*

'So, they're avoiding the icky feeling of being wrong,' I resolved. 'It's pretty fierce that feeling. That heavy hotness is strong; it takes me down. I feel alone with it. Is being different wrong because it sure does feel that way?'

'I know what you mean. When you're different, it's like you're the odd one out,' Harri agreed.

'I feel unwanted,' Aurora looked relieved that somebody else felt like that too. 'I didn't realise other people felt like this. I thought there was something wrong with me.' She unburdened the weight of being different.

'I did too. I want to disappear so nobody could see me. I don't want them to discover my secret wrongness,' I explained. 'I feel small and want to hide away.'

'They might stop being your friend or be horrible to you,' Harri revealed his greatest fear, 'then you will be alone.'

In amongst the chaos of the waiting wishes, we stood close together making sense of the secret wrongness. Nobody is disgusted with us or wanting to run away. Quite the opposite, we were all connecting through sharing our most inner feelings. As we batted our secret stories backwards and forwards, our courage to tell the truth and our understanding for one another dissolved the icky shame.

'I spend so much time and energy correcting it. I try to be what other people want me to be or I try to be right. I want to be a Perfect 10 so people will like me.' *I can see how I'm protecting myself from being rejected.*

'People think I'm confident because I talk a lot, and I'm really good at talking,' Aurora was being really honest now. 'But it's like my insides don't match my outsides. People call me attention seeking when I reveal my hidden wrongness, and they don't believe that somebody like me could ever feel unsure or unliked.'

There is no Perfect 10, Scrowlie's words flowed quickly. *All humans are flawed and all humans feel shame. Being human will not drive people away. The right people will love you without question because you're very lovable the way you are.*

'I didn't mean to lie or trick people,' Harri looked horrified that he'd broken the Wildheart code. 'I thought that if I was like them, they would stop. I guess I'd be better off coming clean about the dancing. I could just zip up my power suit to protect myself from their cruel jibes,' he reasoned.

'That's right! People will have opinions and make judgements about you, but there's nothing you can do about that. What other people think of you doesn't change who you truly are. You know who you are and it's really none of their business,' Nettie affirmed with utter conviction.

CHAPTER 15

WISHES GRANTED

'Let's test it and see which one is more believable. Take it away Scrowlie!' Nettie pretended to hand the microphone over. Scrowlie came forward to take a bow. We all clapped and giggled excitedly. We were intrigued to see how on earth the strength of my belief was going to be calculated.

Your body is an energy measuring tool. Stand up straight, with your feet hip distance apart. Make sure that your toes are pointing forward. Now, take some deep breaths to centre your energy. First of all, we're going to work out how your body interprets the truth. I want you to repeat what I'm about to say and then let your body move in whatever direction it wants to go. Relax and trust that it knows the truth.

'I want to have a go!' Kam popped his head up from under the table. He had started reading one of the Rainbow Books. Nettie firmly closed the book and pointed to a sign which said, 'PLEASE RESPECT PRIVACY'.

She put her index finger to her lips to remind him, 'It's Ruby's turn. Come and watch, so you know what to do,' she whispered kindly. Kam clumsily moved towards Nettie, almost tumbling into The Desire Pit. He had so much nervous energy in his little body that he couldn't seem to settle. Nettie grabbed him and gently pulled him close. He sat in her lap and took her hand like a small child. He looked afraid as he watched on with wide eyes.

My name is Ruby, The Soul Scroll wrote. I wondered why he was asking me to say my own name out loud. Still, I repeated the words and waited. This was unusual for me but I did it! I stood as he had instructed me to and closed my eyes. I had put my hand over my heart to drop out of my busy head and feel into my body. Suddenly, my body swayed forward, and I stopped myself from tipping over. I laughed, shocked that my body had such a strong reaction to my words.

'Well done!' Nettie clapped. Kam joined her in his slightly over-zealous fashion. 'Kam!' Aurora glared at him. She thought better of it and glanced sideways with an apologetic smile.

That's your truth. Now say, 'My name is Zippy! instructed Scrowlie.

I tried not to giggle and remain centred in my body. I repeated the words like before and waited. I closed my eyes and rested my hand on my heart. Then, as if I was being drawn by some magnetic invisible force, my body responded. It was slower this time and it pulled me back onto the heels of my trainers. I stepped back onto my feet to rebalance myself and turned to The Soul Scroll who had already started to scribble, *Forwards is truth and backwards is false. That is your body's measuring style. Now you know how to find your truth when you're doubting.*

'Now do I say my wish and see which way my body goes?' I asked.

'Yesss!!!' they all screeched at once.

I shuffled my feet on the floor and then placed them down like I meant it. I sucked in my tummy and straightened my back like a ballerina. I placed my hand over my heart, 'I wish I had the courage to be myself.'

There was absolutely no hesitation in my voice, and everybody leant forward waiting to see what my response would be. My body swayed but it didn't really go one way or the other. I pulled a face and could feel myself getting frustrated.

'Try again!' Kam encouraged.

I did my foot shuffle try again as if to shake out my energy. I placed my feet firmly on the ground. 'I wish I had the courage to be myself.' This time, I swayed and tipped backwards onto my heels. I clenched my fist with anger. 'Nooo! I want to believe!' I felt defeated.

'When you really believe, you can do anything! No matter what anybody says, don't let that into your heart. Imagine your wish being a tiny seed in the ground. You water it with your belief, over and over. With time and attention it blooms, and you believe your wishes into real life.'

'You can be the tallest strongest sunflower if you believe that you can!' Kam punched the air and nearly knocked Nettie's crown off her head. She grabbed his hand and said nothing. Her smiled soothed him, 'It's very exciting isn't it?!' she empathised.

'I find it hard not to be knocked off my perch by others.' Harri said laughing at Kam. 'Their words become the truth for me, and I lose my way.'

'We can test that too,' Nettie suggested. Harri worked out that his truth was forwards and his false was rotating in a half circle clockwise.

'You look like you're dizzy!' joked Kam. 'It's not the same as Ruby,' Harri protested.

'Funnily enough,' I said to him, 'you're different to me!' We all began laughing at the irony while Harri carefully considered what he wanted to say. He inhaled deeply before saying, 'I wish I could stay loyal to myself when other people aren't.'

His body remained still. Nothing. He looked disappointed and the corners of his mouth twitched. 'What will help me believe more?' he asked.

'Would you be friends with you, Harri?' Nettie asked. He shoved his hands in his pockets and shrugged his shoulders. 'I guess if you like football, you're not going to want a dancer for a friend,' he said. He sounded so sad and hopeless about the situation.

'Freddie wants to be your friend.' Aurora reminded him. 'We adore you, Harri,' she gushed. Harri's cheeks coloured. His cute dimply smile and loving, gentle nature were a joy to be around, but Harri couldn't see himself in that way. His view had been clouded by all the bullying lies he had repeatedly been subjected to in the playground.

'Bust some moves!' yelled Kam. 'Show us what you've got.'

Harri looked down. Embarrassed, he scuffed the floor with his shoe.

'You know, Harri,' Nettie said, 'I think being a dancer is only a part of who you are. You have so many lovely qualities. People who value your kind heart and your generous spirit, will see you for who you are and not want you can do or what your hobbies are.'

Suddenly, we were interrupted as a multi-coloured flurry of books thudded one by one onto the table. It was the rude awakening we needed to get busy again. The shoot had kick-started into action again and another wave of wishes came rushing into the Life Library wanting to discover their fate. We joined the production line and Scrowlie was in charge of delegating tasks.

Aurora can help check for B stamps. Harri can help with The Desire Pit and Kam can file.

Nettie fetched wheelbarrows for us to transport the books to their various homes. Maybe putting things away at home had been my life training for this moment. Nettie asked the

Mermangels to help Harri because she didn't want him to fall in The Desire Pit. She set us all up for success and then bustled off to make tea.

About ten minutes in to our filing duties, Kam started to open and read the Rainbow Books again. 'Kam! You're not helping. They're not your books. Here, swap with me.' Aurora ordered, her tone bossy and clipped. I could see she was annoyed that he wasn't helping. I was a bit too. I took the little pot of Caramella out of my rucksack and smeared it on my lips just in case. I felt protective over Kam like I did with my sisters.

'Nah. I'm bored. I can't think of a wish. I thought I might get some ideas in here,' he leafed through the Rainbow Books and scanned them for wishes.

'Hey! Wishes are private!' called out one of the Mermangels who stopped work to intercept Kam. Unperturbed, Kam skipped off in search of mischief. Scrowlie tried to distract and entice Kam back with his words of wisdom.

Our brain goes towards pleasure and avoids pain, he wrote. *When things are hard or boring and repetitive, we need to find a way to make them fun.*

'That explains why I want treats all the time,' I sighed dreaming about the orangey chocolatey goodness of Jaffa cakes.

'And why I hate homework!' Kam is drawn back into the conversation. He did want to learn, and he was interested, but he was finding the task monotonous and he couldn't focus for long.

Harri volunteered to play some music from his phone, but to our dismay, we discovered that there was no wifi. Aurora suggested singing, but Kam wanted to play. Kam was very restless, and I could feel Aurora's frustration building.

'We just need to get it done, Kam,' Aurora lectured through gritted teeth. Kam hid under the table. His energy was fragmented, and Aurora's words didn't reach him. The more she badgered him, the more he pushed back. They were locked in some sort of power dance where neither one of them would back down.

Nettie broke the tension and appeared at the bottom of the staircase. 'It's R& R time!' she called. She was carrying a tray of goblets filled with rose petal tea and a plate of muffins. Nettie winked at me, 'Rock buns!' she mouthed, delighted to be able to make up for my missed cookery lesson at school. I pulled the face. She smiled, 'No sugar. Wait until you've tried them.' Everybody was grateful to be able to put down tools for a Rose and Rest break. I bit into a rock bun and was surprised by how sweet it tasted. I wondered how Nettie had made them taste so yummy.

'What is in here?' I asked her.

'What can you taste?' she avoided my question. She let me work it out for myself. 'Close your eyes and really taste it!' she instructed. This was a totally new concept to me. We were superfast eaters in our family. I didn't taste my food, I inhaled it.

'It's banana!' Kam declared. He hovered close to Nettie and tugged at her dress. He was like a small child trying to get her attention. She bent down and took his hand in hers. 'That's right. It's mashed banana, Kam. What else do you need?' she gently enquired looking deep into his big brown eyes.

'I want a hug!' he said sheepishly. Smiling, Nettie held out her arms and he nestled into her chest. He was the same age as the rest of us but he seemed a lot younger. I wondered if like Nellie, he had been babied too?

'Are you tired?' Nettie asked Kam as she stroked the top of his head. He didn't answer and closed his eyes. He seemed more peaceful and relaxed when he was close to Nettie. Her calming energy does have that effect on you.

'Why didn't you say?' Aurora scolded.

'You didn't ask,' he lifted his head to answer.

'There's a lot of activity going on in here, 'Nettie quickly diffused the discord. 'It can get a bit much,' she said, putting Kam's overwhelm and Aurora's frustration into words. 'Is anybody else feeling like they need something to help them?' she asked concerned.

I put my hand on my heart and checked in to see how I was feeling. I was hot and I wiped my forehead. I also felt a little anxious because I was keen to file away the wishes. I felt hurried and under pressure like I did when I had a test or an exam. At home things had to be done quickly or in a certain way and that created a lot of worries because you could never be sure if you were going to get it right. I reminded myself that I was doing my best. We all were—even Kam who was safely snuggled with Nettie. I took a few deep breaths of my own, and the angsty feeling began to subside.

'You're doing a great job. I'm so grateful for all your help,' Nettie said graciously.

It was thirsty work and we guzzled our tea. Aurora was quiet and I wondered what she was thinking. She fiddled with her plaits and appeared distracted about something. I asked her if she was okay and she started to tell me that she didn't understand why Kam had listened to Nettie and not to her. As if her help was ignored or rejected.

'Did I do something wrong?' she asked looking sadly at Nettie.

'What do you think? I could see you wanted to get the job done and you were trying to help Kam. There are different ways of helping. How do you prefer people to help you when you're stuck?' Nettie asked her.

'I was quite bossy and I told him what to do. You asked him what he needed. I was annoyed and you were calm.' She looked deflated as she went back over what had happened.

'It's great that you can reflect in that way,' Nettie praised. 'There's nothing wrong with taking charge. When we talk, we're repeating what we know. When we listen, we might learn something we haven't heard before.'

Aurora's face changed and you could see that she loved that idea because it spoke to the part of her that was passionate about learning new things. Wildhearts are energised by deep understanding and love to discover more about the world around them. Aurora told us that her parents were very strict. 'I get told off all the time,' she confessed. They didn't ask her what she wanted, they simply told her what to do and she had to do it. I could totally relate to what she was saying. It's the first time I've really seen her stop, think and listen. I feel for her as being told off a lot feels rubbish and it doesn't really help.

Whilst we enjoyed our petal infused water, we talked more about the difference between telling and asking. As it turned out, we all like to be asked instead of told because that gives us choices. We also talked about how we learnt more when we discovered something by ourselves. Most of the things we were told to do, we did to avoid getting into trouble. We preferred to have the freedom to learn for ourselves. We also talked about being listeners and talkers. Kam, Aurora and I all confessed that we talked more than we listened, but we were paying attention and we did care about what other people had to say. We acknowledged that sometimes it was hard to listen because our heads were so busy. Harri said he was a good listener and often girls would come and talk to him about things that bothered them.

'It's hard to listen when you feel like others can't hear you or they don't believe you. People who can't hear you or don't believe you are often heavily invested in their story and what is right for them. Is it any wonder you want to keep on talking? You are hoping that one day somebody will hear you and believe you.' Nettie explained.

I'm sorry, Kam,' Aurora said.

'You weren't to know Rora.' Kam's new nickname is a white flag and they seem to have reached an understanding. It feels like we're all trying a bit harder to listen and allow the silence.

'All your feelings are true for you. Nobody else gets to tell you how you feel! Sometimes the power of the truth is in our actions and not our words.' Nettie went on. 'When we say less, we can show more. That way, we retain an air of mystery and let people think about it. They can have the time and space to work it out for themselves. I know I certainly learn better that way. The truth has the loudest voice of all. Anybody who is honest and decent will know the truth when they hear it. They will also know when they are being fed a load of rubbish.'

'Do they have different energies?' I asked thinking about how it feels when somebody is not being honest with me. It's a feeling in my tummy and I can instantly see when somebody is lying to me or to themselves. It's a ninja skill I've developed from living in The Hologram House.

Nettie nodded and paused to let me think about it some more. She knows I will ask questions or pull a face if I don't understand. I love the Wildheart curiosity. We like nothing more than to challenge, think big and look at all of the possibilities. Nettie's words were so affirming, I want to record them and listen to them over and over again. She was the one person who believed me. I didn't have to convince her or say very much. I particularly liked what she said about words and actions because that was how it was in The Hologram House—words say one thing, actions do another. How can I match my words and actions? How can I be the one true me, instead of pretending to be all the different Rubies?

'Is it cruel or unkind to tell the truth?' I asked.

'What do you think?' My question was left unanswered in the air. The silences are not awkward or uncomfortable with Nettie. She gives you the time and space to expand your mind and draw your own conclusions. You didn't dread the silence or wait for it to be filled with hurtful words, shouting or even a smacked bottom. Those smacks really stung, but if you were brave like me, you didn't feel them. You tensed up, shut your eyes tight and zoned out. It was all over pretty quickly. I think the anticipation of waiting for the hand to fall was scarier. *Would I get one or two?* On the days when I had been worse than bad, I lost count. Over time, I got braver and I got used to the sting of the smacks. What was more painful was that they came from the hand of the person you needed the most. The hand of the person who you thought really loved you.

'I told a teacher about the boys who were bullying me at school,' Harri confessed. 'It got me into more trouble and the bullying got worse. They called me a girl and said that I'm pathetic because I don't join in and tell tales. When I've tried to play football, they won't pick me to play. It's like I can't win with them. They don't want me to play anyway.' He looked devastated.

'It's not right that they bully you for being different,' observed Kam. 'There's nothing wrong with liking what you like.' Aurora backed him up.

'I love to dance,' I enthused. I really wanted Harri to know I was on his side.

'No matter what anybody else says, it's the right thing to tell an adult if you're feeling unsafe, uncomfortable or hurt,' said Nettie. 'Bullies feel powerful when people are afraid of them. They use your strengths and weaknesses against you which is why you feel like you can't win,' she reassured Harri.

'They do make me feel wrong,' Harri agreed with Kam.

'They make you wrong, so you doubt yourself, and that's when you're fearful. It gives them the upper hand. If you're different, they make you wrong. If you're strong and speak up for yourself, they make you wrong, but really you blow their cover by showing them you're not scared. It's okay for you to be scared but you share your scared with an adult that you trust. Just because a bully says something about you, doesn't mean that it's the truth. Other people's opinions of you are not truths, they are just opinions. You don't have to give them any time, attention or make them mean that anything is wrong with you.'

'Is it cruel or unkind to tell the truth?' I repeated the question and then answered it for myself. 'It isn't cruel or unkind to tell the truth, but it might not be something everybody is ready to hear. In Harri's case telling the truth is kind, it's being kind to him. Why would he be kind to the bullies when they don't have his best interests at heart?' I questioned the bullies' integrity and made them wrong instead of Harri. Harri needed more people on his side. Harri needed to stay on his own side.

Nobody said anything but in between nibbling rock buns and slurping tea, our busy brains were mulling it over. Our energy was renewed from some much needed R&R and eventually, we returned to our librarian duties and order was resumed once more. The Life Library had begun to look more like its old self, glowing in moonflower splendour. The table was cleared of Rainbow Books and by force of habit, I offered to mop the floor and dust the cobwebs away, but Nettie was adamant: 'Dust breeds when you clean it. Let it settle. I think there are much better ways to end our day. We've all been working hard. And besides, it's not doing anybody any harm is it?' Now that kind of truth really was music to my ears.

CHAPTER 16

THE FIRE IN MY HEART

'I hate you!' I screamed at my Dad. We were standing by the fireplace, face to face and inches apart. 'That's *not* what happened,' I protested. The TV in the background was not going to drown me out either. As I hysterically struggled to tell my side of the story, he vigorously shook his head in disgust. He wasn't listening but that didn't stop me. I wasn't going to be defeated. I wouldn't go quietly. I had to make him see that I was telling the truth.

As I raced to finish my sentence, he sucked on his teeth taking a sharp breath in and raised his hand. I saw it come towards me. It stopped by my face and stopped me in my tracks. I didn't flinch or duck this time. I met his gaze. The air was red. The fire in my belly was raging.

'Go on then. Hit me!' I dared. 'Will it make you feel better?' This kind of sass usually upped the tempo, but I couldn't take any more of it. It was the last straw and I didn't care.

His tired eyes flickered, and his hand dropped by his side.

'Get to your room!' His lips barely moved. His teeth and jaw clenched. He stood firm like a Sergeant Major waiting for me to take my orders. The tops of my legs were shaking as my body was preparing to run. I wasn't a fast runner, and sometimes I would escape and hide. I think the others had learnt to be quiet instead of run, but I couldn't keep the words inside.

I stormed upstairs, an angry soldier, hurting the soles of my feet as I made every stair count. I heard the change jangle in his pocket as he sat back down in his armchair. He wasn't coming after me. Nothing was more important than his TV viewing. I imagined him watching the TV, newspaper close by.

Relieved, I slammed the door behind me. Then I kicked it for good measure and made it rattle in its frame. My fists were ready to fight, my breath short and raspy. I let out a cry so ferocious, it echoed around the walls and shook the foundations of our beautiful house.

'You will listen.' I grunted as I swan dived onto the duvet. I buried my face in my pillow and its marshmallow softness kindly held my frustration. I couldn't lay still. The fury made me restless, so I got up and started stomping. I flung open draws and cupboards and slammed them shut again. I gave the door another kick as I loudly searched for something to soothe my white-hot rage.

I climbed up onto my desk and caught sight of myself in the window. 'Uggh! Revolting!' I shouted as I crawled over my desk and onto the glossy windowsill. I caught my leg on the radiator. The burning pain jolted me out of my anger. I sat down and pushed my nose up against the windowpane. My tears fell like rain on the cold glass and my angry breath turned it steamy.

'I hate you,' I wrote in the cloudy condensation with my index finger. I went over what had happened in my mind. I sat with my knees up under my chin, my head leaning against the window. I traced the lead squares with my finger and tried to recall my Mum's version of events and then mine. I felt confused because it was so mixed up in my head. She was never wrong and this is what made it unfair. No, it wasn't just unfair it was impossible. It was her reality or else. She didn't lie exactly because 'Liars always got found out!' No, she was too smart for that. Instead she told my Dad her version of the story missing out all the parts which vindicated me.

I was hangry. Have you ever felt like that? So hungry that you are angry. A bit dizzy and a bit fizzy, it all comes out sideways. Dinner wasn't ready and I was hungry. I wasn't sneaky. I didn't lie. I went to the fridge and helped myself to a strawberry. Can you believe 'Strawberry Gate' exploded into a big drama? My Mum didn't want me to spoil my dinner. I'm not sure one spoiling strawberry was at fault! It was the usual— a mix of my temper and sass, with my Mum's mood swings and stress. I hated it more that she could speak to me exactly how she wanted. I had to sit there and take the shouting and name calling. I wasn't allowed to answer her back.

I felt vengeful and glad I had taken my rose quartz back from under her mattress. 'She doesn't deserve nice things. She is mean and I hate her!' I spat, tears pouring down my face. As the argument peaked, my Mum had thrown her final threat, 'Wait until your father gets home!' Only, at that moment, she wasn't expecting him to walk in mid-shouting match. This wasn't the welcome home he wanted after sitting in a big traffic jam for hours. His face was as black as thunder. I felt as if my strawberry was about to make a reappearance.

The curtain ruffled against the back of my head, it made me jump. I hadn't opened the window. I turned around and there she was. She was holding something sparkly in one hand whilst she used her other hand to take her rucksack from her shoulders.

'Whoah! There's so much sadness here, Rubes' she waved her hands around in front of my face trying to clear the air. 'It's all stuck inside of you. You hold it all in because somehow you think crying is daft.'

'It makes me feel weak, Nettie.' I pouted. 'I need to stay strong so I don't get pulled in by The Hologram.'

'So that's why you're angry huh? It feels powerful to be that mad. It's a strong energy like all your feelings.' Nettie validated my anger. 'What colour is your anger?'

'Red!' I answered. 'Ruby Red. As red as my name. As red as my fiery wild hair. It's out of control.'

Nettie raised one eyebrow and crossed her arms over her dress. Her outfit choice today was a pretty green dress, but it was very creased. *'It could do with an iron,'* I heard my Mum's voice in my head.

'Everybody gets like that.' Nettie said matter of factly as if it was no big deal.

'Try telling that to my Dad downstairs who I've driven to the edge of sanity.' I argued still looking for a fight to release my pent-up frustration and anger.

'If you listened to anger, what would it say? Give it a voice or hand it a pen.' She looked at me, her eyes willing me on. Up until this point, nobody had been interested in or given me permission to talk about my anger.

I pursed my lips and grabbed them with my fingers, twisting them around to lock my mouth shut.

'What will happen if your anger comes out?' Nettie asked watching me writhe and agonise over my feelings.

'Well I know what happens,' I haughtily replied. 'I'm the devil child and I have to be banished to my room because I'm upsetting everybody. It's hopeless. They don't know what to do with me.'

'Do you really think that's the truth, that you're the devil child?' Nettie gently challenged.

I searched inside my mind for the answer. Silence. It felt disloyal to see myself as anything other than devilish. I raised my eyes up to heaven so I could think harder. My tummy growled. I hurriedly spoke over it, embarrassed.

'I don't know,' I concluded hoping that Nettie didn't hear my rumbletums.

'Well something certainly does,' she gestured towards my tummy. 'Does it have something to say?'

I blushed. I wasn't feeling hungry and my tummy was full. I clenched my jaw to try and stifle my tummy which was full of angry horridness.

Nettie watched me. She placed her hand on my back. 'It's okay,' she said. 'Breathe. Let that out. Whatever it is, let it be.'

'It feels so horrid. I feel like this bad person who says and does bad things which upset people. I'm all wrong. I'm so bad people send me away. They don't like me. I talk too much. They hear me because my anger gets their attention. They hear me, but they're not really listening.'

'It hurts to feel ignored.' Nettie showed me she had understood exactly how I felt. It's the same when I snuggle my dolls into their prams with blankets at bedtime. I understand what they need.

'I'm so tired,' I put my head in my hands. I didn't want her to see me upset, but I felt like the human version of Scrowlie, and I knew these words had to come out. 'I try so hard to work out what they need and to be good and kind, but it doesn't last because this takes over and spoils it all ...' my voice broke and my angry rant dissolved into tears.

'It's good to cry. Underneath your anger is so much sadness, Ruby,' Nettie repeated. 'There's a lot which saddens you isn't there?'

'I want them to like me,' I sobbed. 'I don't know what else I can do to get them to like me. I feel so lonely.' The crying turned to wailing as I pulled my knees tighter towards my tummy.

Nettie handed me a tissue from her rucksack. Her gentle voice and angelic smile could melt the angriest of hearts. I fix my eyes on the embroidered 'W' and just stare so I don't have to think anymore.

'You are a mighty Wildheart, but you don't have the power to make other people say, feel, and do things. Nobody does. Other people make choices.'

'They do? Is it a choice?' I pulled a face. 'I thought about telling them, but something stops me. Every time I try to tell them how I feel, or what it's like in here,' I point to my head, 'they get angry or laugh at me. They don't listen to me!' I pushed my hand strongly against my head in frustration.

'Do you think that's a wise decision not to share with them, Ruby? You're listening to yourself and keeping yourself safe from more upset. Sometimes when people haven't learnt how to be comfortable and accepting of *all* their feelings, they criticise, blame and try to control those feelings in other people. They need to see you as this bad kid because then they don't have to look at what they feel bad about,' she explained.

'What I really want you to hear is that there is *nothing* bad about being angry. There's nothing bad about any feeling, they all have their place. When people feel bad about the way they feel, they will hide it or pretend it doesn't exist.'

'I don't want to be '*Show Ruby*',' I cried. 'It's too hard. If I'm not her there are no hugs, no treats, no saying goodnight ... sometimes there's no supper. Without '*Show Ruby*', I'm punished and alone.'

'Who is '*Show Ruby*'?' Nettie was confused. 'Can you turn '*Show Ruby*' off?' she went along with my story. Even though I know I wasn't making much sense to her, I felt like she understood. She looked at me and listened intently.

'She's a fake. She isn't real. I don't really turn her off, not even at home. When I'm *'Resting Ruby'*, when I'm alone or I'm right inside a book or drawing a picture, I can forget about her. I get angry about being *'Show Ruby'*. It all builds up inside of me and then I explode.'

'So, you're hiding how you feel because you don't want to get into trouble and you want people to like you?' Nettie clarified.

'I can't stand it when people don't like me. I feel wrong and bad again. I can't stop it. Angry children get sent away to think about how bad they are. They are punished because they are bad.'

'There is nothing wrong with you, my lovely Ruby. You're not bad. It's human nature to have all these feelings. You need all your feelings to guide you. You must pay attention to them.'

'The only way to be loved again is to say sorry, even when you don't mean it. If you apologise and say it was your fault, even when it isn't, they might forgive you. They like to be right. I worked out that if I lie like they do, if I say sorry, then it will all pass. Sometimes I don't understand what I've done wrong and sometimes it goes on for days and I just want it to stop. So I say sorry. I don't like lying and I don't like saying things I don't mean,' I babbled.

'I understand,' Nettie reassured me. 'I think when we make a mistake or do something to hurt somebody unintentionally we automatically want to put it right. Most humans at their core are good and loving. They have an innate goodness that doesn't require punishment to correct mistakes. We feel bad and this reminds us to make amends. We want to repair the mistake, because we don't want to upset other people. No wonder you're angry if you feel as if you're being forced to say things which you don't mean. You're not being true to yourself.' I nodded my head. She gets it. I don't want to be forced. 'Anger is sadness's bodyguard,' Nettie said.

She's right, I am sad that they want me to do things that I don't feel are right for me. They want what's best for them. I felt calmer knowing this. It made sense. It helped to know she was on my side. Maybe my parents weren't against me. They didn't understand their own anger and weren't able to understand mine. As the anger subsided, I realised it didn't matter who was right or wrong, it just felt good to know that somebody listened and understood.

I thought about the Mermangels and their ability to feel other people's feelings and realised this was a necessary skill if you were going to at least try to understand. If you could try and imagine what it might be like for the other person, it wasn't about who was right or wrong. It was more about relating to each other's feelings. This is where caring and loving takes place.

'Do you fancy coming to hang out with the others for a bit?' Nettie asked.

I tossed my tissue in the direction of the door. 'She shoots she scores!' I yelled and raised my hands up over my head, as my tissue hit the target and tumbled into the bin.

By the time we arrived back in The Wilderness, the others were gathered by the edge of the woodland. A lacey white butterfly circled the flower tops and the birds welcomed me with their shrill melodies.

'Doubt is like a butterfly!' I said to myself. 'It flutters in your mind and distracts you from the truth,' I repeated Nettie's wise words and thought about how when I doubt, my mind goes round and round in circles and takes me far away from the truth. They say the truth hurts, but I think lies hurt more. What could be more painful than being far away from your true self?

I watched JB and Freddie dangling from a branch doing chin ups. They had chosen a big old oak tree with strong branches that spanned far and wide. Aurora and Robyn were standing in the shade of the huge leafy canopy. Even though I couldn't hear what they were saying, their body language was easy to read. Aurora, who was usually very animated with her hands and wobbling plaits, had adopted a new stance, she was standing in the power pose Nettie had taught us. Her legs were hip distance apart and she had her hands on her hips. Her shoulders were strong and her head upright.

She was smiling and nodding while Robyn did the talking for a change. She looked confident, but Robyn was chewing her nails and seemed to be distracted by the boys scaling the branches above.

It looked like Aurora and Robyn had been collecting shells from the walled garden nearby. That's where Harri was sitting on a tree stump looking wistfully into the sky. He'd taken his shoes and socks off and was grounding his energy to the earth just like Nettie showed us. I was learning all these new tricks but hadn't managed to use them when it mattered most. I guess it would take time and practice to do things differently.

I absolutely adored the tranquillity of the walled garden. It was a quiet place to go for thinking time. I would rather be there in the fresh air to enjoy the last few hours of sunshine, than alone in my room with my thoughts. The arched entrance to the walled garden was covered in rambling roses. The floor was paved with pastel coloured cobble stones and the decorative mirrors on the red brick walls gave an illusion of space. In the centre was a tall water fountain made of white stone. Its three tiers reminded me of a wedding cake. The sound of running water was relaxing. It wasn't for drinking, but instead was laced with Epsom salts to clean and calm auras. Epsom salts are not salty at all; they are made from natural minerals and are much more powerful than swimming in the ocean with Shoukey and Orchid.

I must have instinctively known when I washed my feet every night that was what I needed to feel relaxed enough to sleep. Nettie had said running your hands under cold water also calmed you when you had run out of patience. I felt there was so much more to learn that could help me feel better. Why didn't we learn this stuff at school?

The true magic of the walled garden was the clarity clouds. Cloud watching was dreamy. On a sunny day lying in my garden, it was fun to see what pictures or shapes could be created from the cloud formations. The clarity clouds were slightly different. They were a much needed comfort blanket and served as relief from worry. Every now and then, a cloud would pass and lightly restore peace in the mind of the worrier. The fluffy white mist would float down low enough to cover the worrier's head and shoulders. The lightness dissolved any mental chatter. It took with it all those unanswered questions and neverending thought loops that streamed through your mind cluttering it up and weighing you down.

Nettie had taught us how to create a 'Super Sqaud' with our imaginations that would help us when we faced a tricky situation, or wanted answers to things we weren't sure about. It was like having your own personal team of excellent guides that could help you feel safe and supported. All you had to do was call them into your clarity cloud and ask them for help. It reminded me of what Starry had told me about calling her —no phone needed! I had never found this kind of peace from being alone in my bedroom because I was too afraid of what might be happening elsewhere in The Hologram House. Here, in the garden protected by the high walls and soothed by the gentle trickle of the fountain, I felt safe. There were no looming threats or angry parents lying in wait.

As I passed the walled garden, Harri and I waved at each other and I was about to leave him to it, but something stopped me. I wanted to get clear about what I was going to do. What were my choices? Could I put up with life at The Hologram House if I was able to nail the right lessons for my Gold Book? What would it be like to be a Swapsie? Could I create another Ruby —a better Ruby — one who would be a better fit for my family?

I sat down quietly with my back to Harri so as not to disturb him. I kicked off my shoes and wiggled my toes. The lumpy cobble stones were hurting me. I bottom shuffled to a nearby patch of soft grass and resettled myself. I closed my eyes and waited for a clarity cloud to descend. Inside the blackness of my mind, the quiz master had disappeared and was replaced with a softer kinder voice.

'Choose the most helpful people for your Super Squad, the ones who can help you get clear. Call them into your cloud one by one to help you!' the voice instructed.

As I chose each person, their face appeared on the mental screen of my imagination. My body felt light and floaty, and my face was smiling as each one came to greet me. First of all I saw Bert. I had chosen him because he was wise and helpful. Even though it was in my mind, the clarity cloud made it crystal clear that he had a message for me. He was in a Policeman's uniform, I had only seen pictures of him dressed in uniform and was smoking a pipe. He took the pipe out of his mouth and said 'What is true Ruby, for you?' I smiled because 'This is true!' was his response to most things.

Then Bert sat down and started watching one of his detective programmes. We were in a strange room, not one that I knew. Mrs Barnes showed up next. I had asked her to help me because she was very practical. She opened the register and then peered over the top of her spectacles. She said 'Have you got all the facts, Ruby?' It was like being awake in a funny dream.

She sat next to Bert, who stopped watching his programme and nodded. 'Yes, find out all the things you need to know before you make up your mind.' Gloria wondered into the strange room, she had made some rock buns and was offering them around to everybody. She wanted me to use my creativity. 'Ooh, Ruby you write such lovely poems! You're very good with words. Write it all down and see what feels right!' she said enthusiastically. Mrs Barnes gave me her pen to borrow. I could see myself sat on my bed crying, my diary on my lap. I took the pen and started to write. Like The Soul Scroll, I seemed to have a wisdom all of my own. I could see Nettie standing on the windowsill with the Mermangels who were softly chanting. 'Follow your heart!' Tom was curled up on my pillow asleep but it felt safe knowing he was there.

On the page I wrote down my Super Squad questions and then answered each one from my heart.

What is true for you? I am happy in the Wilderness but I love my family.

Have I got all the facts? I don't know what a Swapsie is and I don't know If I want to trick my family because that doesn't feel right for me.

What does my heart say? It wants want is best for me which is to .....

Then out of nowhere, Nellie appeared. I hadn't called her into my cloud. She was in her cot with little podgy hands reaching out to me. 'Up! Up!' she pleaded. A tear trickled down my face. *I couldn't leave her, could I?*

I squirmed. That didn't feel very nice at all. Nellie's face faded away. From the darkness, the voice spoke again. 'This is a fluffy warning. Your cloud will be floating away in five seconds. Five! Four! Three! Two! One!' I opened my eyes and put my hands over my face to shield the strong sunlight. I felt a bit dazed but not confused. I reminded myself of what was important. Bert wanted me to be honest with myself. Mrs Barnes wanted me to gather all the information. Gloria wanted me to be creative with my problem solving. Not forgetting Nellie who wanted me to stay for hugs. She was the snuggle monster!

I had so much to think about, but I had found it helpful to call in their wisdom like this.

CHAPTER 17

THE SILENT DISCO

'Hey, it's Rubes!' Kam greeted me with his cheery energy whilst Gabe stood quietly by. I could see he was on health and safety patrol, making sure that JB and Freddie didn't fall from the tree mid acrobatics. I felt like that when I was left in charge at home. It doesn't leave much room for fun if you take your responsibilities seriously.

'Hey, Kam! Hello, Gabe!' I felt liked by them. It was such a contrast to the greeting I got at the end of a long school day. I could tell Kam and Gabe were genuinely glad to see me and it felt less tiring to be me. I didn't have to worry about summoning one of the other Rubies or pretending to be something I wasn't.

India was with Nettie, pointing at a bush. I couldn't see what they were looking at. As I approached, they continued pointing and talking in hushed voices. I heard India say, 'I think it's my Grandma,' and when I drew closer, I could see it was not a grey haired old lady she was talking about, but a dear little robin. The robin puffed out its red chest and enjoyed the attention. 'I read in a book that whenever you see a robin, it's somebody from heaven who is here to say hello,' India whispered.

I smiled thinking about the robin that sits on my Dad's spade in the vegetable patch and wondered if that's my Nanny too. I never met my Nanny Dolly, but I was often told I smiled like her. She sounded like a fierce Wildheart too, and I wished she had lived long enough for me to find out.

'Nature has so many ways of letting us know that we're not alone and everything is going to be okay,' Nettie explained. 'The wonder of nature is there for us if we notice it. The Moon and the changing seasons tell us when it's time to let go of the old and start anew.'

'What other signs are there?' asked India holding the crystal pendant around her neck.

'Whenever I see white feathers or coins on the floor, I know that all is well.' Nettie replied. 'Whenever a squirrel crosses my path, I know that life has gotten too serious and it's time for fun.'

I hung back, not wanting to interrupt their conversation. I was enjoying the comfort of being with people who were just as fascinated and curious about life as I was. The Wilderness was a captivating place with so much to learn, and Nettie's a great teacher. She was very different to Mrs Barnes. She didn't have a plan, she let things unfold slowly. It was much more exciting to observe, explore and discover things for ourselves without having to rush. It was fun and there was no pressure to remember it all. You can't get it wrong and because you knew that, you paid attention and you didn't forget a single thing.

I think about how much the other kids in my class would love it here and enjoy learning in this way. I also think Mrs Barnes would like to be able to teach in her own way instead of following strict guidelines. A lot can be said for having the freedom to do things in your own way and not feel like you're getting it wrong.

The robin flew away and Nettie and India turned around and made space for me to stand with them.

'Did you see the robin? We were saying how nature talks to us in funny little ways, and how it takes care of us and guides us when we pay attention,' India engaged me in their conversation.

'I was listening. I wasn't snooping,' I looked down. 'I hate it when my Mum goes through my stuff. I really want to learn more about signs from nature,' I added because I didn't want them to think I was being sneaky.

'You're always paying attention,' Nettie chuckled. 'Not much gets past this one!' she said to India tapping me on the shoulder. 'You don't need to know it all today. Let it come to you when the time is right.'

'Yoga helps,' India said readjusting the bracelets on her arm. 'It slows me down. It's so busy at school. Nonstop, and I get quite easily caught up in the craziness with everybody else.'

'Stay in your own lane and let the signs find you,' Nettie wisely advised. 'It could be in a song on the radio, words on a building, a shape in the clouds, a snippet of a conversation that we're meant to overhear, a white feather, a penny that we pick up in the street. Notice and pay attention to the signs. You will discover your own signs and then you can give them meaning, so they make sense to you.' she said encouragingly. We wandered back to join the others and Nettie called us all together.

'Where's Delta?' I asked.

'You'll never guess what happened ...' Kam was eager to spill the beans. Like Aurora, his filter was broken and he couldn't hold on to his words. Although, sometimes mine have a tendency to fall out as if an unknown force has taken over.

'Wait one moment. I know you want to help and share, but is that your story to tell?' Nettie gently reminded him about privacy. She had already told us not to gossip about the other children when they weren't there. 'Only tell *your* stories and how they make you feel,' she had taught us.

'... but I'm doing the heart emoji,' Kam insisted creating a heart shape with his fingers trying to show her that he didn't mean any harm.

'Don't you emjoi me, young man!' Nettie teased.

'Is she okay?' I pressed for more information.

'Yes, she's fine,' Kam reassured me. He put his hand over his mouth like he was trying to stifle the story he so desperately wanted to share. ‘Sometimes, I can’t keep the words inside. Nobody tells me their secrets. I go into my wardrobe and say them out loud. They have to come out. I don’t mean to upset anybody,’ Kam explained. I noticed how I was like Kam, over explaining everything and naturally assuming that people will misunderstand me. A lot of people around me made it their business to misunderstand me, so they didn’t have to be accountable for themselves.

JB and Freddie had taken a break from their exercise and joined the girls at the foot of the tree. Robyn and Aurora skipped around the tree with shells hanging from their ears. They hopped carefully over the solid roots that were breaking through the soil. Harri arrived from the walled garden looking refreshed. Basking in the clarity cloud had made his eyes distinctly brighter and his smile was back. His whole face lit up when he saw that the girls were dancing.

‘Ruby, come and listen!’ Aurora called me over to join her and Robyn. Aurora stopped dancing and held the shell up to my ear. I could now understand why she was bobbing about as the music reached my ears. I wanted to dance too. ‘Welcome to the

Silent Disco!' she announced putting her hands on her hips and giving a little shimmy.

Harri and Freddie were now busting out some of their own dance moves. The wide grins on their faces reflected their mutual appreciation of their different passions—when football met dance. They were snorting with laughter, as Freddie jumped into the air and flicked his head to the right. It looked like he was heading an imaginary football. Harri did the same but his head went to the left. No sooner had their feet simultaneously touched the ground, they jumped up again, only this time, flicking their feet up to touch their bottoms. Next up was a spot of air guitar. Harri carefully showed Freddie how to moonwalk. It was amazing to watch Harri skilfully back slide his feet over the grass and end in a spin.

'The boy's got moves!' Freddie nodded his head in time to the music and pointed his index fingers at Harri. You could see Harri's heart was swelling with pride and having the courage to let his guard down was worth it. It was written all over Harri's face, 'A footballer is taking dancing lessons from me!'

I loved to dance, but I was a controlled dancer. It didn't come naturally to me the way it did to Harri. I am self-conscious, stuck in my overthinking and petrified of making a mistake. *Why couldn't I loosen up and let go?* I wondered as I watched Harri and Freddie's delightful performance.

From a young age, I had listened to Motown and Beatles classics. I had sung along and knew the words by heart. Even though I didn't fully understand what they meant. I played instruments. I made up songs. I choreographed shows for my parents, and I sang out of tune to the radio. I loved music because my performances made them notice me, but I guess I hadn't fully appreciated its true expression. It was so much more than a song. It was a message spoken with real emotion and passion. Each song had a purpose and a message. It gave a voice to love and heartbreak. It inspired joy and sadness. It expressed hope and courage. I guess I couldn't truly embrace the fullness of its magical energy because I was too busy keeping a lid on how I felt and who I was.

It's true, I could be a better dancer, but it's not a risk I was prepared to take. In my dancing classes there was a glaring audience, and on occasion, a dance examiner ready to judge and score me. I mostly liked to freestyle it out in my bedroom, but the performance other people saw, left them saying things like, 'Ruby could be much better if she was more confident in her ability.' It's the wrongness at work again—my outsides didn't match my insides.

I could be confident when I had to be. That's *'Show Ruby'* at her finest! I knew how to smile, how to speak up, how to give them that razzle-dazzle. It took effort. It didn't come naturally to me, but I'd mastered it, like I'd mastered most challenges that life had chucked my way. Anyway, true confidence is more than jazz hands, it's a deep feeling of knowing that you are accepted just as you are, and if you aren't accepted, you know that you would still be okay. I didn't feel accepted and I didn't know I was okay.

I am riddled with shame. It's not the slight embarrassment when I'm shushed. It's not that guilty twang which motivates me to correct my wrongdoings. It's not that dragging heaviness I carry with me when I get it wrong or make a mistake. It's not the voice-stealing- terror that leaves me frozen when I'm being screamed at, reprimanded or pummelled over the head by angry fists. No, it's far worse than that. *'That's a bit melodramatic!'* my Dad's voice filled my head. No, it's a thick, black treacle that has infiltrated my very being, poisoning my blood and breaking my heart. The ugly cloying stickiness holds me trapped. I am stuck between choosing myself or choosing *them*. What kind of a stupid choice is that? Before I was born, had I signed a contract with the Karma Fairies to sacrifice myself, and my place in this family to protect them from their pain?

This, deep-rooted, toxic shame forces me to betray myself and leaves me abandoned in the darkness. I am alone, but not truly being myself. I do not belong with them either. We are all washed up in a no man's land where nothing is real and yet appears to be perfect. Everything we could have been has been eaten alive and destroyed by shame.

If *'Rageful Ruby'* is wrong, bad, mad, and nasty, how come she is the reason I'm still here fighting for my voice to be heard? She may get me into trouble, and she may be the reason I don't like myself very much, but I won't let go of her because she saves me from totally losing my true self. The icky black shame feeds the lies. It controls my behaviour and edits our stories. It blocks my feelings and it robs me of my joy, my innocence, my hope and my self-belief. Bit by bit, it had tried to take me down, but *'Rageful Ruby'* had kept my Wildheart spirit alive. She fought valiantly for her place in the world. Her spirit was fierce with the strongest will known to man. In the deepest darkest waters, it would never sink. It would always find its way and swim.

How could little old me be the one thing that knocked my family out of balance? I pondered. It was most definitely out of whack, but it wasn't much to do with me. My family was sick, and the shame held it hostage. The real me needed to stay hidden, cast away like a dirty secret. It was exactly the same for Harri—he was the music. The rhythm was in his soul and running through his veins, but the bullies had shamed him to keep his true self locked inside.

Nettie and India shouted, 'ENCORE! ENCORE!' repeatedly as they gave Harri and Freddie a rapturous applause. Off they went again with their funky routine, both blissfully lost in the music. As part of the audience, we can't hear it but we can feel it through them. It's powerful, the emotional expression of music combined with the love of a friendship based on radical acceptance. Cruel judgement and fear couldn't survive it. Harri had discovered the confidence to really shine like the incredibly talented dancer he was.

The swirly shell earphones, despite their delicate nature, were surprisingly comfortable. The beat of the music pulsed directly into my ear and rippled through my body. The electrifying energy shot to my feet and sparked them into action. Unable to resist the powerful force, I tentatively stepped left and then right. I tried to remember my set pieces from dance, and my mind went blank. I put my hand over my heart and inhaled. I let the music in. I closed my eyes and let go of my plan. Step ... two three four ... step. I felt the rising crescendo willing me on to freedom. I nodded my head and punched my fist into the air.

Cocooned inside my shell ear defenders, it was safe enough to let it all out. With each and every punch of my clenched hands, I was fighting back and I could feel the simmering anger from earlier. The rushing fire rose up with the strong bass line. It felt justified as I stomped my feet firmly into the soil, determined and strong. The drums took on the booming voice of my anger that desperately wanted to be heard. The injustice of it all, the hurt, the sadness, were finding their voice. It validated every truth I had ever wanted to speak and shattered every lie they had ever told.

It relentlessly pounded into my ears forcing me to listen. Nobody was there to push it away or hold it down. Nobody could tame it or make it wrong. It was all mine. I wanted to be with it because I could get to know it better. I could understand it and help it. I could do for myself what others had failed to teach. The grin on my face was huge and a warm glow radiated from the middle of my chest. It was safe and secure. I think I had just turned up my heart energy. I guess it didn't feel so bad to me after all.

The sun set like a big glitter ball in the pink sky. It was getting colder, but the music had fired us up, and given us permission to tell the secret stories inside of us. I looked around at everybody lost in the moment. Anybody watching would have quite rightly thought that it was utter madness to be rocking around the hillside in silence with shells hanging off our ears.

Finally, we sat down to rest on the grass—hot and tired from our workout. Harri was the last to join us, his fingers still snapping in time to the music. Something had awoken in him and it felt like it wasn't going to stop any time soon. I felt much taller, there was more space inside me to breathe.

JB laughed, 'My family teases me so much cos I sing silly words to songs and get them wrong.'

'My family just loves to make me wrong,' I chipped in sarcastically.

Nettie grinned. 'I don't think you need to know the words, the music speaks for itself,' she observed. 'Why do you think little babies who cannot talk yet, are soothed by lullabies? It's a Universal language like love. It is an invisible force of nature that breaks down the barriers of fear and judgement.'

I wiped the sweat from my forehead and pushed my fringe back in place. I looked over to check out Aurora's plaits, they were frizzy and dishevelled, but she looked delighted. Her cheeks glowed pink as she sat next to Robyn in their little bubble of friendship. Robyn was preoccupied with a rabbit she had spotted twitching in the undergrowth. She sat patiently willing it to draw closer.

'I'm Mr Wrong!' said Freddie loudly. He stood up. 'They call me Wrong. James Wrong,' he gave us his best 007 impression. He tipped his cap to us with one hand and scanned the audience with a smoking gun he pretended to hold in the other. Aurora raised her finger towards her lips to stop him from disturbing the rabbit, but she couldn't hide her amusement. We all began laughing. The rabbit hopped away.

'Songs remind me of places I have been to or times I've shared with other people.' Harri relished in this conversation and you could see how music truly was his thing.

Freddie started to sing the theme tune to James Bond whilst making gunshot sounds. Harri and Freddie really were quite the double act and I was happy for them, but also quite jealous. I wished I had that special connection with somebody who got me without having to say very much. It would certainly feel less lonely. Freddie listened to Harri, 'I love to play songs over and over again, especially the ones that feel good. Music can make your heart beat again when you think you've run out of energy. When you think you can't do it anymore, you step into the music and let it revive your soul. It takes over your body and everything is good again.'

CHAPTER 18

THE FEEL-GOOD CAMPFIRE

As we chattered away, nighttime crept up on us. Nettie lit a fire. The orange flames burnt away the scary darkness and we all huddled around. It was so easy to share with Wildhearts. These were my people and it felt like we had known each other for all time. There was nothing to hide or pretend. Scrowlie and some of the Mermangels joined us. I was really pleased to see Starry again. She had brought food with her and knitted blankets. We snuggled down for more storytelling and laughter. I wriggled around to cover up my sandals which were peeking out from underneath the red blanket. I like to be covered up with woolly jumpers and scarves. I think that's why I like the cosiness that a rainy day brings. It feels safe and secure.

'What happened to the others?' Starry asked looking at my sandals.

'They didn't make it. They didn't make the cut—they weren't white enough,' I joked. She laughed. She knew that I meant my Mum had binned my yellow encrusted plimsolls. At least, you could say that she was consistent with her unwritten rule—anything that became tarnished was banished. That wasn't reserved for shoes and inanimate objects, it was also the same for feelings, differing opinions, friends and children. Her children.

'Have you decided yet?' Starry asked me. I knew what she meant but I didn't want to think or talk about it. It had been playing on my mind. I couldn't get peaceful with any one of my choices.

I was saved by a rustle in the bushes. It was Delta. As she appeared, I could see that she looked crushed. Her arms weren't folded, and instead her shoulders were slumped in defeat. 'I didn't do it,' she said as she broke into a sob. We all looked at each other shocked. It was most unlike her to be so openly emotional.

'Come!' Nettie stretched out her hand and drew Delta in to join the gang. Our energy was still high from our musical madness. Together we stood strong enough to hold Delta in our huddle hug. Kam repeatedly swallowed and was visibly uncomfortable with the level of crying. Freddie and Harri had sat down and busied themselves with unnecessary tasks—retying shoelaces and awkwardly rolling up their sleeves. There was some very strange coughing now coming from Kam who was wrestling with his own feelings.

India and Aurora tried to meet Delta's gaze with their kind eyes and warm smiles. Robyn bit her nails and I felt as if I wanted to say or do something. I found it so hard to see somebody in pain and not be able to do anything. The hopelessness and helplessness of not being able to make it better was uncomfortable, but I could see that Delta was hurting too. Nettie was unruffled and held the silence in the palm of her hand. She had this amazing ability to stay neutral and calm in the face of any emotional storm. And yet she wasn't detached and uncaring. She remained open and let Delta be with her sadness. It was what was needed, and I had never thought it was possible until I had experienced the same soft, kind energy which had held me when I was overcome with emotion. Delta put her head on Nettie's shoulder and Nettie stroked Delta's hair.

'It's okay,' she said. 'Things get hard sometimes. You can do hard things. We're right here with you.' Then she turned to me and said 'Empathy,' as if she was reading my thoughts. 'From loving silence and acceptance, comes empathy,' she whispered.

Nobody spoke but we nodded our heads to show we were on Delta's team. The reassurance of feeling supported, allowed her to say what she needed to.

'I HATE IT!' her tears became angry. 'There is NOTHING I can do! NOTHING!' We didn't know what she was talking about, but we leant forward and kept nodding like we understood. It was like the lyrics to the songs, we didn't need to know what they meant but if we listened carefully, we could hear the music of Delta's true feelings. I saw Gabe put his hand over his heart. Then India did too. I followed suit and did the same. We were all beaming heart energy to Delta.

'Why don't grown-ups talk about the difficult stuff?' she despaired. She was desperate for answers to take away the tears. I knew what she meant—we do a lot of sweeping the difficult stuff under the carpet in The Hologram House. I'm pretty sure my Mum has hoovered under there as well, just to be absolutely sure she has destroyed all the evidence. Delta was right. Why was it so hard to talk about and look at the difficult stuff?

'I'm not stupid,' she spat furiously. Her jaw was clenched, and her humiliation burnt hot whilst seemingly unnecessary to her. She didn't say what, but strongly felt she could have done something to stop it. Whatever 'it' was that had caused her so much pain and upset. Her feelings were big and powerful, a little scary. I mentally zipped up my power suit, but also wondered if that would stop the heart energy from reaching her. I don't think so. My power suit is there to stop energy getting in, not positive vibes radiating out.

'You feel as if you should have known. How could you have known if they didn't tell you?' Nettie comforted her.

'He left. My Dad left last night, and nobody told me he was going. I didn't get the chance to say goodbye.' She was making more sense now. We were a patient audience, letting Delta fill in the story in her own time. Our loving silence gave her more than any words of comfort ever could.

'I know he will think that I don't care about him. I do! I could have made him stay. If he knew I cared about him, he wouldn't go,' she reasoned.

'Why didn't they tell me he was going? I hate them. They are so mean and selfish.'

I'm not quite sure who *they* are, but I assume that she is talking about other members of her family. It's like she wants to blame anybody but her Dad. Making herself wrong is second nature and much easier. All the Wildhearts do this, we protect our parents or others from their flaws. It's strange how we're more accepting of their imperfections, than they ever are of ours. It's okay for others, but for us to be imperfectly human is totally unacceptable.

'It's not their fault. He could have hung around to tell you the truth!' Kam had caught her anger like a virus and was now stating the truth about her Dad's cowardice. Delta wasn't ready to hear it. I agreed with Kam, but I also empathised with Delta. I took deep breaths and stayed silent. For now, I would hold on to my anger. It didn't feel like it would help Delta if I got worked up too. It got me thinking about how I was running out of time. *Was it fair to leave without a proper goodbye?* I constantly questioned if I was doing the right thing. Seeing Delta so upset wasn't filling me with confidence to become a Swapsie. I still wasn't entirely sure I understood what it was.

'I don't know if I will see him again. I don't know if he will come back. I wish I could have told him,' she rattled on, berating herself with her coulda-woulda-shoulda. She couldn't listen, our words didn't reach her. She could only be with her raw emotion. She continued, 'I never thought he would go. I think they could have stopped him. Nobody else tried to. I wish I had told him how I felt before now,' she said regretfully.

'This isn't what you wanted,' Nettie didn't try to change Delta's story. If anything she was more interested in showing Delta that she understood how she felt.

I thought about the difference between sensitive feeling people and the rest of the world. Shallow people, or 'Surface Skaters' as Nettie liked to call them, don't and can't go deep, but instead try to fix you to ease their discomfort. They stay on the surface, they aren't concerned with how you feel. They are only concerned with the story and the drama. That's when they get to play judge and decide what is right and wrong. Of course, they have to be right at all costs. Sometimes the price is high. When they realise they can't fix you or change it, they make you wrong. Yes, that's right—you're wrong for having too many feelings. You're wrong for being a human being who is having an appropriate amount of feelings for the crazy they are putting you through. If that's not bad enough, they want you to 'get over it' because it's time now, and they get to decide when they've had enough.

That's why nobody likes you because you're so over the top! was on replay in my head. Sometimes if I pressed shuffle, I would get *Are you stupid?* It's not a rhetorical question, more a statement of fact. The spite and malice cut me down to size, leaving me helpless. Forever being told when to speak and when to be silent, protecting The Hologram at all costs. *You never know when to keep your mouth shut*. All topped off with the most hurtful one of all, *You make me sick!*

Pffff, I mentally tutted and raised my eyes to heaven. *As if* they *get to decide when it's time for you to feel your feelings and work out what's right for you! It's such a load of rubbish*. I can see so clearly now why my Mum wouldn't have really appreciated me leaving the rose quartz under her pillow. It's not what she needs. She doesn't need to be made happy, she needs to feel and work out her own kind of happy. I'm doubtful that she ever will, but part of me always hopes that she will. That's what keeps me there. That would be the only thing that would stop me from becoming a Swapsie. If I had hope and I believed that was an option, I would stay. It wasn't my choice to make.

'I know how you feel Delta,' my voice wobbled as I found the courage to speak up. 'I'm a bit of a hedgehog when it comes to my true feelings. You have to make it past my spikes and go carefully, because I feel deeply.'

'I'm a hedgehog too.' confessed Kam. 'I'm less of a hedgehog here than when I'm at home.' *Ah, so he wasn't a Swapsie. Was he still travelling backwards and forwards like I was,* I pondered.

'Some of the most caring people in the world have feelings as wide and as deep as the ocean. Their hearts love passionately all the way to the Moon and back, and then back again,' Starry added flicking her long hair over her shoulders.

'I would rather stay and fight. I can hold onto my anger for so long. My family thinks it's being stubborn, but Nettie has taught me that I have determination and that's strength.'

'I find it hard to say goodbye.' Harri joined in. 'I will hold on long after it's finished. Even though I know that the friendship isn't happy anymore.'

'Me too!' I felt relieved that goodbyes were hard for the others. 'I try harder to understand people even when they're mean. I try harder to make people feel better. I'm determined to find a way because in my mind, there is always a way.'

'Yes, Ruby. There's always another day, another choice!' Starry agreed. 'There is always more hope, more love and more sunshine after the rain. There is always a choice to find more of those things, if you want them.' I watched her and Nettie wrapping bananas in silver foil to toast over the campfire.

'It can feel scary to bare your heart, so you have to choose the right people. Not somebody who is shut down like a Surface Skater,' Aurora sounded like she knew what she was talking about.

'I get it Delta,' I smiled at her. 'So many times when I have spoken from my heart, *they* shut me down.'

Feelings are not right or wrong, they are simply energy passing through your body with a message for you. That's what Nettie has taught me. I am piecing it all together now and it's starting to make sense. Watching Delta was helping me to see that none of us are too much at all. 'We're in touch with our most sensitive parts, with our feeling selves,' I shared. 'Where we go wrong, is that we are expecting the impossible from people who can't meet us in that place.'

'It's like trying to order a meat dish in a vegan restaurant!' joked Freddie in his very sweet effort to lighten the mood. *Wow, India would have something to say about that*!

India appreciated Freddie's sense of humour. 'Others cannot give you what they don't have inside of them. It's like squeezing orange and expecting champagne to come out!' she made a little joke of her own.

'You're looking for what you need from people who can't give it to you. It's not their fault, but start shopping elsewhere! I can only love you as much as I love myself.' Nettie told us. 'How much I love you does not equate to how lovable you are.'

I watched Delta emotionally thrash about as she struggled to come to terms with all the feelings that arose from being left without warning. I could sense her overwhelming fear, her insurmountable frustration, her raging anger and her deepest sadness. I could relate to the strong denial that defends her Dad and is protecting her from pain. Admittedly, I wanted to give her some of my unfailing hope, but I didn't want to lie to her. I didn't want her to waste time waiting and hoping that someday her Dad would return. I knew she was way too lovely for that. I don't want her to hold on like I had been, patiently waiting like a 'good girl' for *them* to catch up. Her Dad may never fully know her true colours. He may never meet her where she is. It hit me hard —and my Dad may never meet me where I am. There! I'd seen it now. Would that be okay for me to live in a world where my family didn't understand? I understood now. Was that enough?

It makes sense why Delta folds her arms to keep her guard up. She appears not to care but she does. She really does care. We all do. She is protecting the part of her she thinks she needs to hide. The part of her which is misunderstood, the part of her that needs to be changed, put right. Exactly like Harri did with the bullies, like I did with my anger and Freddie did with his jokes and humour. None of us are wrong or bad for being who we are.

'He isn't coming back, and I don't even know where he is,' she cried harder. Mistakenly, she believed she had lost her Dad, but her Dad was not lost, he chose to leave. He made a choice to steal away in the middle of the night without telling her.

He chose not to talk about the difficult stuff and say the sad goodbye.

'What a coward!' exclaimed Kam. Delta's anger was certainly catching. Kam was right. It was her Dad's job to say goodbye properly. Nobody could have made him do that apart from him. I'm angry too that her Dad had left her with an unspoken goodbye which had broken her heart into pieces. I don't think I could ever do that.

'Other people's choices aren't about us —even though they can hurt us,' Nettie explained. 'Lots of people fear goodbyes. The thought of calling time on something they are not ready for means that if they don't say goodbye, they can leave the door open.'

We sat in silence contemplating what that meant. Kam piped up again: 'That's so selfish. It's all about him and his sadness, what about Delta? Look at her! She doesn't know what's going on.' He'd make an excellent lawyer, you'd want Kam on your legal team.

'Can you trust, Delta, that your Dad loves you enough to return?' Nettie asked her. 'Can you trust that he will always be your Dad and love you in his own way?'

Delta thought about it and wiped her nose with the back of her hand. She sniffed and finally said, 'No, I can't. I can't feel his love when he is far away.'

'Close your eyes,' she instructed. We all shut our eyes and Nettie told us to imagine a cord of energy coming out from our hearts and connecting to each member of our family. Each cord is your connection to them which can never be broken. Even, when there is distance, the cord gets stretched, but the love is always there.'

'Your parents made you,' she smiled. 'You came from them and their energy lives in you, and all the energy from their families too.' Everybody was holding their hearts and feeling into the energy Nettie was describing. It was overwhelmingly huge, and I couldn't understand it. Maybe I wasn't meant to. I tried to sit with the energy instead of work it all out.

When we opened our eyes again, I couldn't stop my question from coming out of me. 'If you're a Swapsie won't you be rejecting your parents? I felt silly for asking and my cheeks coloured.

'What if it's more about deciding about what feels best for your soul? What if your decision is not about hurting anybody or being mean? Do you remember the experiment we did? Your soul knows what it needs.' She placed her hand over her heart and gave it a little pat.

'Switcheroo! Switcheroo! Whatcha gonna do?' sung Kam. He knew! He knew that I was considering it because he had to make that decision too.

'It's not Switcheroo,' JB corrected him. Kam smiled. 'It's a Swapsie. I am a Swapsie,' he proudly revealed. That's why I look like a pixie with these. He pointed to his pointy ears!

We all stared at JB, waiting for him to tell us his story. He swallowed. 'My soul was hurting so much. I mean it wasn't hard to leave because I didn't have anybody to leave. I was left in a doorway when I was a tiny baby. My heart was broken and I was freezing. I never knew who my Mum was. The pain of never knowing her was crushing for me,' he sighed.

We all looked at him. He was so brave. No wonder he felt so grown up. He knew how to take care of himself from the moment he was born.

'The old lady who found me took me home and fed me. She was a sweet soul but her time on Earth was nearly over. She handed me over to a Policeman and that's all I remember.' He looked at Nettie.

'That's right. You won't remember when the swap is made. The soul that replaces you won't remember either. It may take a while for the new soul to settle in your body. We bought you here to The Wilderness, but you were too young to learn lessons for your Gold Book,' Nettie explained.

'Can't you have two families?' Kam asked. I could see where he was going with this line of questioning. He wanted to travel backwards and forwards instead of having to make the decision. Maybe he didn't want those pointy ears!

'You can have as many families as you wish. Family isn't always the people who made you. The Wilderness is my home. This is my family.' JB concluded.

I felt sad and happy all at once. I had a family and I wasn't satisfied with them, but JB had no family to begin with. I couldn't imagine my life without them.

After what felt like forever, Freddie broke the silence. 'It's nice to see you Delta. We've missed you today. Harri's been teaching me how to dance,' he spoke softly, but you could see that he wanted to cheer her up. 'You know, I really didn't think I could dance until today.'

Delta looked across at Freddie and the corners of her mouth turned. Nettie passed her more tissues and she wiped her swollen eyes.

'You can do hard things,' Harri told Freddie as they went in for a high five. 'You can dance, and you can do anything you want to do. You can even start again. You get to choose!' he scanned the group. It felt as if their happiness was another wave of energy coming in to hold hands with the sadness until it had passed.

'Now who wants bananas with cream?' Nettie was plating up the squishy sweet fruits and topping them with whipped cream.

'MEEEE!' we chorused as we passed the bowls around the circle until everybody had one.

'What?' said Freddie putting on a very straight face as he stared at us. He was pretending that he didn't know that he had cream smeared all around his mouth. You couldn't keep a straight face for very long when Freddie was around. His energy was contagious and our hysterics could be heard throughout The Wilderness. Our faces scrunched up and as the laughter made its way into our little bodies, it took us by the shoulders and shook them up and down.

'You look like Father Christmas!' exclaimed Kam. 'Ho ho ho!' it was Freddie's turn to laugh.

When the laughter had passed, the energy felt calmer. The sound of the fire crackling, the warm glow lit up our smiling faces. Nettie had placed a basket of large autumn leaves in her lap and I secretly hoped she was not going to make more tea with them. Or worse, get us to eat them. They looked quite big and crunchy.

'The full Moon is nearly here. It's a time for letting go. It's time to release the stuff that is not working for us anymore. We can let go of people, places, things, feelings and thoughts. I want us all to think about what we'd like to let go of,' she announced as she passed the bowl around. 'Take a leaf and take a moment to think about that.'

I thought about letting go of making myself wrong. Whatever decision I made, it would be right for me. That was what mattered. One by one, we whispered what we wanted to let go of into our leaves. Then we threw them into the fire and watched them burn away.

'Now there is more space for your New Moon wishes,' Nettie smiled as Harri was the last one to burn his leaf.

'We have another two weeks to think about those,' Starry chipped in.

The Moon face in the night sky shone down on us. I think there is a man in the Moon because if you look closely, you can see his face. Before now, I had thought that he was lonely up there all by himself, but now I could see that he had the stars for company. I had found my stars too. I knew how special it was to have met my Wildheart friends.

CHAPTER 19

FOLLOW YOUR WILD HEART

So that's how we arrived here. It's quite a story, but it's far from over. Thank you for listening. I hope it helped you. It certainly did me because I believe that when we share our stories it's comforting to know that we're not the only one. We're not alone and there is nothing wrong with us. There is definitely nothing wrong with you! We are all humble humans trying to find our way home, to the place in our hearts where love lives.

I stand on the patio with Nettie by my side. 'Is this a dream you want to keep alive?' she asks me.

'It's more of a nightmare,' I joke.

'Is this a nightmare you want to keep alive then?' she asks. As we look up at the house together, the pigeons strut on the roof somehow managing to escape the clutches of the wire.

'It's not my nightmare.' I argue. 'How did I end up here?'

'Step out of it then,' she urges me. 'Set yourself free.' She takes a step to the side and invites me to do the same. I think about the Silent Disco and how freely I was able to step easily in time to the music. I desperately wanted to follow the beat of my own drum, although now standing here and looking at my parents still rendered me unable to move. I am still helplessly and hopelessly stuck.

I look at Nettie, confused. 'Make your own dreams! You can do hard things' she echoes Harri's wise words.

'What about them? I've failed them.' I point towards the house.

'You haven't failed anybody. It was never your job to create happiness for somebody that wanted to stay miserable. Maybe they like living the nightmare. Perhaps they feed off the drama or get something out of it. They must do, otherwise why would they stay stuck? You don't have to be like them. It's safe for you to be different. It's a chance for you to unstick yourself.'

'I have no idea.' I shrug my shoulders. I think about how the drama keeps the nightmare of The Hologram House alive. Where there is drama, there is an angry child who is the problem. It's a cover up for the truth. These parents are not a mere victim of circumstance. This angry problem child who bears the blame is not and cannot be responsible or accountable. These parents are the co-creators of their own nightmare. In the name of love, they hand over their pain to their unsuspecting offspring. These angry problem children love their parents and would do anything for them. They will tolerate the lies, they will lie for them, forget about their mistreatment and punishments. They will do anything except what they need to do, bite the hand that feeds them. Freedom comes at a high price. What is an innocent beautiful sweet child to do?

'Perhaps they don't realise they have choices to do it differently. Different is big and scary. It's an alien planet they don't care for. They aren't likely to visit it much if the risk is too high. Remember, they can only get it right or wrong. Different would open up a whole new world to them and set them free. They don't have the courage to take that risk. The helping hand is outstretched. It calls, 'Take me!

Come with me, I know a place where there are feelings, there are colours, there is a light brighter than your darkness that will set you free.' They are afraid and they push the hand away.'

'Is it possible to create my own dreams whilst I'm living in the nightmare?' I ask.

'Did you ask your cards?' she points to my rucksack. I take the cards out and give them a shuffle. 'I forget I have all these things to help me,' I confess.

'Don't push the hand away!' she smiles. 'We all need a little help sometimes. Without taking the hands, we're stuck. Can you reach out and take your own hand?' she asks. 'Can you help yourself first?'

'Amazing things happen to me all the time!' I read the card out to Nettie. 'Well that's just not very flipping helpful at all is it?' I snap sarcastically. 'This is by far the least amazing thing to ever happen to me ever.' I flip the card over, and it tells me to make a wish. I throw it down.

'Make a wish for you, Rubes. Anything is possible if you want it enough. Put your time and effort into creating your own dreams. Stay in your own lane and let others do the same. It's more fulfilling, believe me, than spending a lifetime trying to stop the nightmare. The Hologram House is out of control and like you've just told me, it's not yours to begin with.'

I laugh. 'It feels wrong to leave it though. It feels like somehow I didn't do my job properly.'

'Who ever said it was your job?' Nettie exclaims. She makes a cutting motion with her hand across her neck as if she wants to behead whoever they are. 'I'm firing you!' she jokes.

'I'm the eldest ... I have responsibilities. They're counting on me.' My pathetic attempts at explaining why I don't want to let go are merely echoes of The Hologram's evil lies. It's irrelevant because I'm starting to realise that I'm entitled to live my life as I wish. 'I need you to give me permission.' I find myself asking Nettie. This is new and slightly odd because usually I'm much happier to work it all out by myself.

'I can't do that, sweetie. This is about you. It's not for me to tell you what feels right. Not what is right or wrong but what feels right for you. Can you let them be right in their own way, and you can be right in yours? What would it feel like if you were both different? What would it say about being different in your Gold Book?' She asks all the right questions.

'I don't know. I still feel wrong somehow,' I admit. The feeling is still there, like a distant rumbletum, it serves as an unwelcome reminder of my wrongness.

Being different isn't about being wrong, weird, bad or crazy. It just means you're different. We're all different.' Nettie tells me. 'Find people who love your differences, not people that want you to be like them. There are hundreds of people like that. I call them Sheeple!'

I laugh again. 'Sheeple!'

'Yes, the Zombie Sheeple.' She stumbles towards me with her arms outstretched and does some crazy mad sheep sounds. She does make me laugh. You have to laugh sometimes because this stuff gets really heavy and comedy moments like these make it more bearable. 'They follow the heard, they go with the flow. They do what everybody else is doing but they are never happy because what somebody else wants is not usually what you want. Sheeple are life's true tragedies because they never get to be who they are. They live for others.'

She continues, 'Mmmm, it's not a lesson for the Gold Book yet. Being right or wrong is totally irrelevant. You cannot simplify a person in that way.

Humans are complex feeling beings. They have layers, they have scars, and they have stories to tell. Everything you've learnt won't ever leave you, but it has become less scary now that you understand.'

'It's less scary now you understand!' I tell her as she skips off down the garden. I follow her as she heads towards Snowy's shed. 'Here we go!' she says taking an envelope out of her rucksack. 'Read that later. It will help you decide.'

She chats on about how much Robyn would love to meet Snowy someday. I take the envelope and notice she is shifting awkwardly from one foot to the other. Her energy is slightly jumpy and different than the usual calm steadfastness she brings. I notice her put her hand on her heart. I do the same.

'We're on your team, Rubes! We're all rooting for you. Every single Wildheart and Mermangel is cheering you on. We want whatever you want. We're never far away.' She is jumping up and down, waving her other hand in the air. The other one is still firmly holding her heart. I feel her excitement and then I notice her swallow, 'I have to go lovely Girl!' she rushes over the words.

'Thank you!' I hug her tightly. I don't doubt a single part of who she is, from the top of her purple flowery crown right down to her little silver sandals. I feel so grateful for what she has shown me—patience, constant kindness, endless understanding, and a listening heart full of love.

‘Ok,’ she softly whispers, straightening herself up as she releases herself from my tight hug.

It’s hard to let her go, but I know it’s time. I know our beautiful stories are linked forever and like all stories, they’ve had a purpose. No matter how big or small, each story has earned a place in my Gold Book. Some stories had happy endings and others sad, some of them unfinished and some of them still unwritten. Each story blessed with characters who slowly introduced me to myself. They held a mirror up to my strengths, my weakness, my fears, my shame, my guilt, my talents and motivated me to be the truest version of myself. To all the parts of me which made me human, my true technicoloured self.

I hold the envelope in my hand and observe how strangely calm I feel. The rights and wrongs are replaced with contentment. I don’t have to be tough anymore. Just like Harri and Freddie, our unusual and rather unexpected connection had made it safe to be me.

‘Okay,’ I repeat.

She steps back and my gaze meets hers. My hands are still outstretched from our embrace and I watch her heart glow every colour of the rainbow. Her brilliance illuminates every single fibre of my being. I feel her warm glow and then all at once, she is gone.

I shut my mouth and put my arms back down by my sides. Snowy scuffles in his hutch and the musty shed smell of dry soil and weed killer abruptly brings me back to the moment.

'See that, Snowy!' I tell him, 'that's love right there!' I go outside and sit down on an upturned bucket to read Nettie's final words to me.

My Dearest Ruby,

This is the goodest of goodbyes. I am only a call away but it's your time now. I'm so glad we met. I'm so glad I got to know who you really are. I think you know yourself a little better now too. I know you will remember all the important words, but if I have not said them before, I will say them here and now.

I've loved watching you blossom from the scared girl who held on to everything so tightly, to bravely venturing into the unknown to uncover the real Wildheart inside. Your courage and determination are limitless. I've seen you abandon and doubt yourself over and over again to keep others happy, but you always return. You return to yourself. Every time you did that, you deepened your trust. In a world full of Sheeple Zombies, I know how being loyal and staying with yourself is hard. But it's where you'll feel happiest – where you can feel most like you.

This isn't the end, it's the beginning for you my lovely Girl. You've worked hard to carve your own path. Sometimes doing things that are good for you are not always easy, but you must always do what is right for you—follow your heart! I've often felt the depth of your extreme loneliness. I've watched you isolate yourself too many times, fearing you may hurt others with your anger. You're not like them; you couldn't hurt a fly. I've watched you frantically search for yourself in the eyes of others. I've seen you panic when they couldn't see you either.

You didn't disappear, you were never lost, but they tried to crush you. They tried to ground you down to dust. How foolish to think they could crush someone with a Wild Heart as big and as beautiful as yours. You may be small, but you are mighty, and the power is in your hands. You can be there for yourself now. Be your own best friend and you will never be lonely.

And I know you will make your own rules. You know what's real and what matters most – what you feel inside your heart. You can do that with your heart full of love. That beautiful energy goes beyond all the stars and the planets. It's an infinite energy source which is with you always. Put your hand on your heart and it is there. It's where all the answers are. It's where the truth lives. Your truth. What is real for you is how you feel. Not what is right or wrong. None of that matters—only how you feel inside.

What you've learnt gives you solid foundations for a beautiful bright future. Now is the time to take that, and make it work for you. Use your curiosity to learn more. Keep feeding your passion for learning. It is contagious. Whilst I know many of your discoveries have deeply hurt you, and it may not all make sense now, there are lessons beyond this which will make up your Gold Book. Like the alchemist you are, you'll turn those hurts into lessons, and you will share them with others. Your light will send the darkness back where it belongs.

Remove the word mistake from your vocabulary and give yourself the gift of freedom to explore. Let go, so you can enjoy learning without worrying about the outcome. Life is a true adventure to be lived, not graded or scored. You cannot be too angry, too sensitive, too smart, too ... anything. There is magic and messages in all of your feelings. There is power in anger, there is bravery in fear and there is healing in sadness.

It was never about right or wrong. Somewhere in the middle of black and white, in the middle of right and wrong is different. We're all different. Meet yourself there and get to know all the parts that make up the whole of you. You are a Ruby—a bright dazzling jewel born to shine light into a very colourless world. Don't be afraid to show them that's who you are. Being you is more than fine. You have so much to offer the world. Don't hide any of it away. Not one single bit.

Trust that you're always exactly where you need to be and everything is unfolding as it needs to. You were born to be all that you can be. You don't have to survive a black and white world. Instead, you can sprinkle colour wherever you go. Those who find your light too bright will fall away back into the darkness from where they came. Let them go. They are not meant for you.

Surround yourself with like-minded souls who leave you feeling most like yourself. You get to decide who stays and who goes. Make choices and fill your life with anything that lights up your heart. Every choice you make has consequences. Do whatever makes your heart sing. You are joy.

Every day you get to choose how that day will feel for you. You're in charge and you get to decide. Choose to be happy and kind over being right. There is nothing in right or wrong. It does not connect, it does not seek to understand, only to be understood. Besides, nobody gets to tell you how you feel or what you think. That is yours and yours alone. You get to decide how it feels to be you. Hold on to your truth because it's yours, because it's real and it matters.

You will create magic with your kind words and beautiful smile. Use your gifts wisely. Shine your bright light wherever you go. Leave moonflowers on the hearts of others, so they may expand their light too. Share your hard-earned wisdom to wake up others. You will instantly recognise a Wildheart when you meet one. You will feel the fire within them, and you will not be afraid of it. Let your people know who they are. Hold a mirror up to their strengths and remind them when they are lost that they have their own special brand of magic too. Show them how big your brave is and you will inspire them to do the same!

Protect yourself from the darkness. Meet your fears as many times as you're able and let others fight their own. Hold their hands and be their friend when it gets hard. Hold on tight and encourage them.

Let them find their own way and remind them that they can do hard things too.

Hold on to your hope. In spite of everything, you've never been without that cheery hope that is now building the bridge to your future. Here's to your wishes, dreams, and new beginnings. Fill those Rainbow Books with whatever you want. You've climbed the highest mountain and now it's your time to enjoy the views. The world is yours and you deserve it all.

Her neat handwriting signed off with 'in truth and love'. She always turned the dot over her 'i' into a heart. She filled up the rest of the page with hearts and kisses.

I wipe the tears from my eyes and fold up the letter. I carefully put it back in the envelope and place the white paper over my heart. The unbreakable connection was still there, holding me safely and lovingly. I was okay just as I was. That was the only truth I needed to know. I look towards the house, and then higher up into the sky. Never have the clouds made it clearer. I take a deep breath in and zip up my power suit. I don't have a plan, but I do have love, and I know that whatever happens, I will be more than fine.

A white feather drifts down from the sky and lands at my feet. I bend down and pick it up. Smiling, I put it inside the front pocket of my rucksack, the embroidered 'W' winks at me. An image of the card I had chosen earlier flashes through my mind and the words echo in my ears, 'Amazing things happen to me all the time! Amazing things happen to me all the time!'

My mind and heart are synchronising. Magic is being made as the dots are joined. It makes perfect sense to me now. It's a handsome reward for being brave and patient. I had managed to sit with the not knowing without it gnawing away at me or making myself wrong, bad or dumb.

And it had taken a long time. There was no more time to waste. Amazing things were happening to me and had happened to me. I had survived them all. And more importantly, amazing things were the *making* of me. Amazing things were the making of The Only Ruby I was clearly destined to be.

'Wooo hooo! I'm a Wildheart!' I yell confidently to the trees. As they rustle with applause, I know it's one for my Gold Book. The energy moves down to my dancing feet. I'm back! Freedom is mine as I boogie my way across the perfectly manicured lawn home.

Wilderness Words & Meanings

Aura — Sometimes called an energy field. An energy that shines from each person and can be different colours.

Clarity Cloud — a low floating cloud which clears the mind of worries and helps make decisions.

Clear quartz — a clear crystal that brings clarity to the mind, healing and can help with study or homework.

Epsom Salts — special salts that are dissolved in water to cleanse the aura.

Full Moon —The full Moon is when the Earth is between the Sun and the Moon. The full Moon always comes about two weeks after the new Moon, when the Moon is midway around in its orbit of Earth, as measured from one new Moon to the next. A full Moon is the only moon phase that shines the whole night through.

Gold Book —a record of each Wildheart's life lessons.

Heart Energy — life force energy that is activated by placing both your hands over your heart, closing your eyes and breathing deeply from your tummy.

Intuition — the part of you that knows before your brain does. A bit like having an inner SatNav that tunes you in to your feelings and guides you towards what is right for you.

Karma Fairies — a group of fairies who are in charge of deciding what happens to people depending on the intention of their actions and behaviour.

Life Library — the place where all the Rainbow Books and Gold Books are sorted, filed and stored.

Mermangel — a cross between an angel and a mermaid.

Moon Cycle — this is the different phases of the Moon that take place over 28 days. The phase of the Moon is how much of the Moon appears to us on Earth to be lit up by the Sun. Half of the Moon is always lit up by the Sun, except during an eclipse, but we only see a portion that's lit up.

Moonflower — like a daisy with a purple centre which glows violet and powers up heart energy. It's also used as a light in the Wilderness.

New Moon —The new Moon occurs when the Moon and the Sun are on the same side of Earth. The Moon is between the Sun and the Earth and therefore lost in the glare of the Sun. We see the side which is not lit, so the Moon appears dark to us.

Power Pose — a strong stance that boosts up confidence.

Power Suit — an imaginary body suit to protect negative energy coming into the wearer's aura. The wearer can still beam heart energy outwards when wearing the suit.

Rainbow Book — a record of each Wildheart's wishes.

Rose quartz — a pink crystal that radiates love, compassion and kindness.

Rose Petal Tea—Tea made with rose petals often served as refreshment after hard work.

S&B *(Spray & Baby wipe)* — a method Ruby and her sister Jemima use to clean their clothes quickly without having to hand them over to their Mum to be properly washed.

Selenite — a milky white crystal that helps connect to the true self and inner magic.

Soul — the energy and essence of who you are. Your inner spirit and magic.

Soul Scroll (Scrowlie) — A magical and endless roll of parchment paper that is accompanied by his trusty partner: 'The Feather'. Together they share words of wisdom with Wildhearts to enrich their life lessons.

Super Squad — A personal team of excellent guides created and called upon using the power of your imagination. The energy of these people will keep you safe and support you when you've lost your way.

Surface Skater — A shallow person who is not connected to their feelings. They only look at what's on the surface. They don't talk about feelings. Instead, they gossip about people and create drama. They like to play judge and decide what is right and wrong.

Swapsie — A soul that crosses over to The Wilderness because it struggles to be happy in the family it is born into. The family and friends do not know this has happened because the physical body doesn't change, it's only the soul that is swapped.

The Hologram House —A house of secrets and pretence where Ruby lives with her family.

The Desire Pit—a hole in the corner of The Life Library where wobbly wishes are kept until the next Moon cycle.

The Nook —An underground hideaway where Nettie lives and the Life Library is located.

The Wilderness— a place of stunning beauty where Wildhearts have fun roaming wild and free!

Vibration (*Frequency*) —the energy of somebody's thoughts and feelings can be high or low depending on the feeling. Some feelings like fear have a low vibration, whereas joy and love have high vibrations.

Wildheart — A strong-willed, sensitive child that is in tune with their feelings and the feelings of others, they have a big heart full of love. They are also a creative change maker that leads from the heart with fiery courage and steely determination.

Wobbly Wishes — new Moon wishes that are not ready to be granted because the wisher has a lot of doubt around them.

About the Author

Often called The Smiley Coach, Lisa Parkes is an experienced Life Coach who works with children aged 7 up. Lisa gives them life skills and practical coping strategies for life's hiccups. She has helped hundreds of children become self-aware and develop a positive outlook on life; beating their fears, worries and stresses about homework, exams, friendship struggles, bullying, nerves, and anxiety to name but a few. Lisa is passionate about helping children feel great from the inside out. Her creative coaching workshops and private sessions help children develop self-belief, positive thinking, and most of all to find their own way without judgement in a safe and trusted environment. Lisa is also the creator of Smiley Thought Cards; positive affirmations which encourage emotional intelligence and connect families with love.

Come and say hi on Facebook or Instagram!

Want to be like Ruby and learn how to become your most confident self?
To find out more about Lisa's fun and creative online coaching programmes for parents and children, visit www.smileyforlife.com

Want to connect with Smiley Lisa?
You can find Lisa chatting about all things growing up over on her awesome podcast, *'Truly Madly Smiley'*. There are lots of helpful episodes on tricky friendships and dealing with your big emotions. It's so important to learn how to take good care of yourself so you grow up feeling happy and confident. You're worth it!

Want to become a Wildheart VIP?
Get the free monthly Wildheart newsletter where you can receive blogs, podcasts, eCourses, videos and gifts to help you feel gorgeous from the inside out! **Sign up here** www.smileyforlife.com/dear-wildheart

Please help other children find this book so they can learn too!

If you leave me a review on Amazon, then more children will get to find out about this book! I want to help them and I know you do too. I would love to know what you think, so be sure to leave me a review.

Printed in Poland
by Amazon Fulfillment
Poland Sp. z o.o., Wrocław